FORTUNE'S WAY

FORTUNE'S WAY

Evelyn Hood

041837

WILLIAM KIMBER · LONDON

First published in 1987 by
WILLIAM KIMBER & CO LIMITED
100 Jermyn Street, London SW1Y 6EE

© Evelyn Hood, 1987
ISBN 0–7183–0669–4

Typeset by Scarborough Typesetting Services
and printed and bound in Great Britain by
Biddles Limited, Guildford and Kings Lynn

To Margaret Williams

I

Supported by her father's arm tight about her knees, Rowena felt like a child-goddess above a bee-swarm of humanity that seethed and buzzed and continually changed its pattern as she watched.

Beyond, she could just see the water in the canal basin, Paisley's latest marvel.

'A godless scheme,' Rowena had heard a neighbour say to her mother that very morning. 'An invention of the devil. No form of transport for decent folk!'

'An invention of clever men, like the spinning wheel and the loom,' Morag Lindsay had replied blithely, brown eyes dancing with anticipation of the trip to Johnstone by boat later that day.

Widow Bothwell gave such a disapproving sniff that Rowena thought her long thin nose was in danger of inhaling itself.

'I'm telling you, Mistress Lindsay – no good can come of it—' she prophesied darkly, and retired to her own house.

'Mother—?' Rowena, who at eight years of age had been taught all about the evils of sin at the dame school and the Sunday School class she attended, looked up with sudden misgivings, but Morag laughed and hugged her daughter.

'Pay no heed. You'll see, sweetheart – we'll all have such a time on the new canal today!' she said, and Rowena was swiftly reassured.

The man-made stretch of water between Paisley and Johnstone, some four miles away, had only been opened four days earlier, on November 6th, 1810. Ewan Lindsay, always one for change and excitement, had decided then and there that he and his family should spend their Martinmas holiday on the tenth of that same month sampling a canal trip to Johnstone.

'I want the bairns to be able to tell their grandchildren that they were among the first to take to the water,' he said, and kissed his wife while Rowena and her brother Neil looked on. Unlike most Paisley children, they were used to affection. Ewan, a lean red-headed Highlander who had brought his weaving skills to Paisley some fifteen years earlier and had since become store-man to Fergus Bain, thread manufacturer, saw nothing wrong in demonstrating his love for his wife and children.

Now, clutching at his shoulder, watching the horses that pulled the boat plodding in from the tow-path at last, Rowena rubbed her chin against her father's curly hair and revelled in his reassuring strength.

The gig's bow appeared, nosing its way slowly into the basin, and she bounced with excitement, causing Ewan to protest 'Watch what you're about, lassie, or you'll have the two of us stretched on the ground!'

'No chance of that,' Morag hugged her husband's arm with one hand, and kept tight hold of nine-year-old Neil with the other. 'A body could die and be kept upright in this crush.'

Morag Lindsay was considerably smaller than her husband. From where she sat Rowena could easily look down on her mother's broad-brimmed bonnet, feathered and beribboned. Much as she loved her father Rowena secretly mourned the fact that she took after him in looks, instead of her lovely mother. Morag's heart-shaped face, framed in shining black curly hair, was as pretty as a rose as she tipped her head back to smile at her daughter. She wore her best patterned silk dress over a red quilted petticoat, with coloured silk stockings, and a warm cloak about her shoulders to guard against the November chill. The neat little hand she had slipped through her husband's arm was snugly covered by a quilted muff.

Ewan Lindsay was a conscientious worker and a thrifty man, and his family were all well dressed. He himself wore a blue cloth coat with shiny gilt buttons, cut low to show a white ruffled shirt and black and white striped silk waistcoat. There were silver buckles at the knees of his brown nankeen britches and on his sturdy leather shoes, and his stockings were of good wool.

Rowena and Neil were dressed like their parents, she in her best yellow gown beneath a blue cloak, a ribboned bonnet curtailing her red curls, her brother in a green coat that set off his dark looks well, though it did little to give added colour to his pale face.

'Let me up — let me see!' he clamoured above the noise.

'You're too heavy,' his father objected.

Morag immediately took Neil's part, as she always did. Rowena knew that she had her mother's love, but never as great a part of it as Neil had. She had accepted from babyhood that her brother, thirteen months older than she was and afflicted, like so many children in Paisley's damp air, with chest troubles, was her mother's special pet.

'Not much heavier than Rowena — come down, Rowena, and let your brother up to see the boat.' But Rowena clung to her perch and shook her head. She adored her older brother and normally she would do anything for him. But not today — she refused to be relegated to the ground, where she would see nothing but backs and elbows.

Although she had her father's colouring, while Neil was like his mother, it was as though they had exchanged eyes. Rowena's were deep brown, like Morag's, while Neil's were of the same vivid blue as his father's. Now they glared up at her and his mouth took on the familiar petulant square shape it adopted when he was crossed.

'I'll take him, Mistress Lindsay—' a voice offered eagerly. Kerr Fraser, known only vaguely to Rowena as a lad who worked in Watson and Bain's manufactory, stood directly behind Morag, square face flushed and eyes bright with his anxiety to please.

'He's far too heavy for you!' Morag protested, but already Neil was swarming up the youth's sturdy frame and onto his shoulders, almost knocking Kerr's three-cornered hat off. Morag retrieved it and reached up to replace it as Kerr wriggled Neil into a more comfortable position.

'I can manage him fine—' he said breathlessly, and Ewan added, as his wife was about to argue further, 'The laddie's got strong shoulders, Morag — and a willing heart too, I'll be bound,' he added with a chuckle.

Kerr, still trying to regain his balance under Neil's weight, didn't hear the last words, but Rowena saw Morag's elbow dig into her husband's ribs, felt the laughter shake him, then saw her mother turn to give her beloved son's benefactor one of her most radiant smiles.

Ensconced on his new perch, Neil stuck his tongue out at her, but she didn't care. All her attention was on the boat that had wallowed ponderously to a standstill in the little canal basin.

The *Countess of Eglinton* was a serviceable single-cabined vessel, built to convey a hundred and fifty passengers. From her vantage-point Rowena could see that the deck, with its long seat running down the centre, was thronged with passengers who had made the journey from Johnstone and were waiting to disembark. From her perch she saw that the crowd seethed and surged with excitement. There was something deliciously dangerous about such a mass of people, and such a noise, when she was safe on her father's shoulders. Her hands moved from his glowing hair to lightly clasp the sides of his lean face.

'Stay close to me, Morag.' She could feel his voice reverberating through his cheekbones and into her palms and up her arms to warm her heart. Her mother obediently tightened her hold on his arm, at the same time retaining her clasp on Neil's hand.

With difficulty, because of the crush of folk, the little gangplank was put in place and the Johnstone people, grinning self-consciously, aware of their new-found importance as seasoned water travellers, began to come ashore. The waiting crowd pressed forward, those in the front jostling onto the gang-plank as soon as the last foot left it, heedless of the harbour-master's instructions.

'In a line, now — there's room for everyone. If the ladies and gentlemen already on board would be so good as to go into the cabin and make way for the others—'

To her annoyance Rowena saw Neil go before her, turning to grin back in triumph as Kerr thrust himself through the crowd. Morag, determined not to lose contact with her son, followed close behind. A group of youths reached the gangplank immediately behind her and began to fight their way on board, forming a wedge between Ewan and his wife.

Rowena felt his shoulders lift beneath her thighs as he took the sloping plank, then they were aboard the *Countess*. She saw Neil disappear into the crush as Kerr lowered him to the ground. Her father, calling to his wife and son to follow him, was trying to make his way to the other side of the boat, away from the gangplank. But the youths who had boarded before them blocked the way as they stopped to look back and jeer at the people still trying to get on board. Many others who had managed to get onto the boat did the same. Rowena saw her mother's bonnet bobbing amongst the crowd.

'Get back—' Her father echoed the harbour-master's shout above the babble of voices. 'Daft fools that you are — get back and balance the bo—'

Then a hundred-voice scream shrilled to the sky as the solid deck tilted sharply beneath the crush of passengers, dipping the low rail beneath the water, throwing those nearest it into the basin. The empty, unbalanced side of the boat lifted clear and the deck became a precipice down which men and women and children slid helplessly.

To Rowena, it was as though the people and the sky suddenly moved out of their proper place as her father was thrown to one side, away from her. Hands flung out to catch at a support, mouth agape in a scream of animal terror, she felt herself cart-wheeling through the air and glancing off something hard that hurt her shoulder. Then there was the shock of cold water on her skin, water that weighed down her best clothes and filled her mouth and nose and eyes.

Panic-stricken, lashing out with arms and legs, she surfaced as the boat tossed the last of its passengers from its deck and slapped back into the water, floating upright now that it had regained its centre of gravity. The water between boat and harbour was lashed to dirty foam by people struggling to reach the bank. Mistily, Rowena saw a few heads and arms at the cabin windows as those who had gone below reached out to drag others to safety.

Then the wave created by the boat's return to an even keel surged towards her, bringing with it a clutter of bonnets and gloves and umbrellas torn from their owners. Her clutching fingers closed tightly on one of the umbrellas, but it couldn't hold her on the surface. With a despairing cry that turned to a gurgling struggle for breath she went under again, her head pounding like the drum the weavers marched to on celebration days and when they had a grievance.

She could actually see the great drum being carried along Causewayside Street, gleaming blue and gold in the sun, its mighty voice proclaiming the pride and determination of the Paisley weavers. Silken banners bellied out in the wind, straining against the poles that held them at each side. Somewhere, she knew, the fifes were shrilling, but the noise was muted by the sure, steady beat of the drum in her ears. Although he was no longer a weaver her father was marching with the others, his red head making him easy to see, his blue eyes sparkling with life and vitality.

Crushed painfully by the crowd, unable to breathe, she tried to reach out to him, but her arms were heavy and strangely reluctant to move. The drum-beat grew louder and all she could see was her father's red head growing larger and larger while everything else began to slip away as though into a mist.

A hand caught at her hair and tugged, roughly handling her and throwing her onto something hard. Rowena tried to protest, but coughed and choked instead. Foul-tasting water gushed from her mouth and her stomach heaved until there was nothing more to choke on.

The noise of the drum had given way to the piping of the fifes; this in its turn yielded to voices screaming and sobbing in the harbour basin. She opened her eyes, and found that it hadn't been a bad dream after all.

She was lying on the hard harbour stones; feet and trouser legs and skirts hurried to and fro around her. From where she lay she glimpsed the *Countess of Eglinton*, riding high and half-empty in a basin still lashed to foam as survivors tried to help the drowning.

'Mother—' she said weakly, then mounting terror gave strength to her voice as she looked round for her family. 'Father — Neil!'

Hands gripped her shoulders when she tried to struggle to her feet.

'Stay where you are.' Kerr Fraser tried to hold her, but she refused to heed him.

'Where's my mother?' She fought against his restraining hands, screaming for her parents, finally sinking her teeth hard into his wrist.

He let go and she was up, stumbling on the stones, tripping over someone who lay stretched on the ground, almost falling, but staggering on towards the water's edge and the screaming bedlam there.

To her horror she recognised a gleam of green and gold in the muddy water near the bank — Neil's jacket, its gilt buttons winking at her.

He was so close that she could kneel down and catch hold of his collar. She pulled, and the sluggishly floating body swung towards her, black hair eddying about a white face as it came. She tried in vain to lift him but he was too heavy, and she would have toppled into the water beside him if Kerr hadn't gripped her and dragged her to safety for the second time.

All about them people were busy pulling others ashore, trying to revive them, calling and searching for their own folk. It was left to Kerr to gather Neil in his arms and lift him clear of the harbour. Brushing Rowena aside, he held the boy up by the ankles, shook him hard, and didn't stop until Neil choked, spewed canal water, gasped, and began to cry.

Kneeling beside him when he was laid down again, Rowena was aware for the first time of the chill November air striking through her wet clothing, the sodden bonnet still clinging to her bedraggled head. She tore it off and threw it away as Kerr lifted Neil in his arms and stood up.

'We must take him away from here—' he said gently, then his eyes moved to somewhere behind her, and he added with a new urgency. 'Somewhere else — we'll take him somewhere warm, you and me—'

But Rowena had already turned to see what had caught his attention. It was easy to spot her father's red hair, even among the great mass of people who wandered about, weeping, or lay unmoving on the stones, or worked feverishly to revive those dragged from the water.

Ewan was on his knees, his good Sunday clothes dripping water, his ashen face lifted to the sky, his mouth open in a soundless cry. A motionless bundle, also dripping canal water, was clutched in his arms.

Unable to comprehend, for the moment, what had happened, Rowena started towards him, but was stopped by Kerr's hand, tugging her away from the harbour, out into the street, where word of the tragedy had spread and the crowds were already gathering.

II

'Fergus, I want those children!'

Sarah Bain's childish voice always deepened to a hard, mature note when she was determined. Her pretty mouth was set firmly against opposition. As she crossed to the elaborate fireplace, soft, virginal white muslin drifted in a cloud about a body that was still youthful despite her thirty years.

Above the mantel hung a portrait of herself and her husband painted in the first year of their marriage. Sarah took up her stance below it. The *Paisley Repository*, which had just been delivered, lay scattered on the carpet round Fergus's chair, where it had fallen after being plucked from his hands by his wife's impatient fingers.

'Their father surely has first claim on them—' he began.

'Their father's near out of his mind over Morag's loss.' She crossed her arms across her breasts, hugging herself tightly. 'Poor Morag. To die like that! Crushed under all those folk, drowned with no way to reach the surface—'

'Hush now, Sarah! There's nothing we can say or do to get her back. Her suffering's over, poor soul. She's safe with the Lord now.'

'And it would make her salvation complete if she knew her children were being well looked after.' Even in her grief over the death of the young woman who had been both maid-servant and confidante during the early years of her marriage Sarah knew how to take advantage of Fergus's natural generosity. She dropped to her knees by his chair, tilted her carefully groomed pale-gold head back to look up at him.

'Fergus, you know as well as I do that Ewan Lindsay's not in a fit state to see to those children. When he isn't at the store he's sitting alone in his cottage. All he can think of is Morag. I'm told he's not as much as asked after the children. If it wasn't for that neighbour of his taking food in every day and seeing that he ate it he'd have let himself starve to death by now.'

'Aye, you're right,' Fergus admitted. 'I've tried to speak to him about it myself, but it's as if he can't hear anything, unless it's about his work.'

'If it wasn't for us the bairns would be dead of neglect – Neil for certain, with that pneumonia he got after his soaking.'

She reached up and cupped his face in her hands. Fergus Bain was twelve years older than Sarah and usually as indulgent as the doting father who had reluctantly given her to him in marriage.

'Ewan's been one of your best workers for many years, and if you remember, I wept when Morag married him and left us. And—' she added softly, 'you know it's always been my great sorrow that you and I weren't blessed with bairns of our own—'

'I never knew that worried you over much, Sarah.' His voice was a trifle dry, and her blue eyes blazed at him for an instant before being subdued beneath long silky lashes.

'It did, though I never let on. I always felt I'd failed you in that way, Fergus. It's my delicate constitution that's to blame. But now there's children beneath our roof to make our lives complete. A wee girl for me to care for – and you could train Neil to go into the business.'

'Sarah, you go too far too fast! They're only bairns, and they're Ewan Lindsay's bairns at that!'

'I know, I know—' she said swiftly, soothingly. 'But it's more than likely Ewan'll want the boy to follow him into the mills anyway. And don't you see, Fergus, that we'd have a ready-made family, you and me?'

'Your tongue's running away with you, woman. What happens when Ewan comes back to his old self and wants his bairns where they belong, under his own roof?'

Sarah's eyes met his, wide and innocent. 'When he does I give you my word I'll be happy to return them. Would you rather have the man searching through the Poor's House for them? Is that the sort of employer you are, Fergus Bain?'

He opened his mouth to protest, thought better of it, and gave in. 'Have it your own way, woman. You always do.'

'Oh, thank you, Fergus—!' Then Sarah was hurrying across the big room to the double doors, her small slippered feet making no sound on the thick carpet.

'Sarah!' His voice stopped her as she opened the doors. 'Mind, now — they're only here for as long as it suits their father. Don't you go spoiling them.'

She smiled radiantly at him over her shoulder. 'Oh, I won't—' she assured him, and swept on across the wide hall and up the great curving staircase to the next floor.

Left to himself Fergus rose and stooped to pick up the sheets of newspaper, grunting gently as he did so, made aware of his thickening waistline.

He put the pages together and folded them tidily before going to the big windows that looked out over the neat lawns and sweeping driveway.

The comfortable mansion house he and Sarah shared was situated at Carriagehill, on land gently sloping up from Paisley, the Scottish weaving town that was at that moment the centre of the flourishing shawl and thread industry.

Thick rhododendrons at the bottom of the lawn hid the town from his sight, though above the shrubbery he could see smoke from its chimneys eddying in the grip of a cold late-November wind. Off to the right, on the other side of Hunter Hill's green mound, flowed the canal.

Not far beyond it was the River Cart, and less than a mile along its banks stood the thread manufactory of Watson and Bain, run by water-powered machinery. John Watson, Sarah's father, was long dead, but his name remained over the mill gate.

In that direction, too, about half a mile away from the house, lay the basin where Morag Lindsay had been drowned two weeks earlier, together with eighty-six others. Most of the dead were young; most of them, like Morag, had been pinned to the bed of the six-feet deep basin by a great crush of panicky folk.

Fergus groaned softly at the thought and his fingers clenched on the watch chain looped across his rounded stomach. He himself was a founder member of the Canal Company, and one of its major shareholders.

The *Countess of Eglinton* was running again. Already the tragedy was a thing of the past and passengers were beginning to flock back. There had never been a pause in the carriage of goods since the *Countess* started plying. Fergus expected to make a fine profit from the canal.

His thoughts moved to the children upstairs. Sarah was right — Ewan Lindsay was a good employee, and Fergus had a responsibility towards the man's motherless family.

It would be pleasant to hear young voices in the house, there was no denying that. And it was important to keep Sarah happy. After all, it was through his marriage to her that he had gained the thread manufactory.

There was another reason why he had given in easily to her desire to keep Ewan and Morag Lindsay's children, a reason that nobody, least of all Sarah, would ever know.

Fergus was well aware that he was thought of in the town as a dour man, difficult to get to know. He often wondered what his neighbours — even his wife — would say if they knew that beneath his gruff manner lurked a shy romantic soul.

Fergus himself looked on it as a character defect. He groaned again as he allowed himself the rare luxury of recalling the one person who had, quite unwittingly, wakened that inner romantic. Gentle, lovely Morag Lindsay, his wife's maid when they first married, had captivated him from the first moment she set foot in the house. It had been both a delight and a torment to be under the same roof as Morag. He had experienced searing jealousy and overwhelming relief when she left to marry Ewan.

If Fergus had known of young Kerr Fraser's adolescent passion for Morag it would not have surprised him at all; she had been everything a man sought in a woman, and it was to his eternal sorrow that he had met her too late. Her death had affected him deeply but the prospect of her children coming under his care, even for a few short weeks, was balm to his grief.

A twinge of rheumatism lanced painfully through his right knee, breaking his train of thought. He returned to his chair, picked up the *Paisley Repository*, and settled down to read.

*

Singing to herself, Sarah went up the stairs, past the paintings of

Paisley views that, like the house itself, had been her father's wedding gift to her, and along the broad upper hall.

Her housekeeper was coming out of the last door.

'How is he, Mistress Cochrane?'

'Doing well enough, ma'am. He took some gruel an hour since, and his sister's reading to him now.'

Sarah was bursting with her news. 'Mistress Cochrane, the master and me have decided that we'll care for the two of them — until their father's able to take them back, that is.' Then, as the housekeeper's face chilled and her lips parted, she added hastily, a placating hand on the other's wrist, 'Of course I'll hire a nursery maid at once. But I depend on you to help me to see to things. I could never manage without you — as you well know, Mistress Cochrane.'

The older woman visibly thawed. 'As you wish, ma'am. I'm sure it's a good Christian thing you've taken on, looking after the poor motherless bairns.'

She went off along the corridor and Sarah opened the bedroom door. There were two beds, for Rowena had refused to be separated from her brother. The room was as large as the ground area covered by the entire Lindsay cottage in Common Loan, with windows that looked out to the back, to the kitchen garden and small orchard and, beyond the stone wall, to the braes that rose behind Paisley.

Neil, so fragile that a breath of wind could waft him away, lay back on piled pillows, his silky dark hair brushed back from his pale face. Rowena, in her newly-laundered best gown, the one her mother had dressed her in for the canal trip to Johnstone, her red hair tied with a ribbon of Sarah's, sat in a chair by the bed, reading aloud slowly from a child's story book on her lap. Her faltering voice stopped as Sarah came in.

'Mistress Cochrane says you're a lot better.' Sarah leaned over the bed, let her fingers brush that lovely soft dark hair. Neil smiled up at her, a trusting smile that made her heart turn over.

'We'll be able to go home soon,' Rowena said.

'When Neil's quite strong again.' Sarah looked at the two of them, seeing them anew now that they were hers. Despite what she had said to Fergus, she had never grieved over-much about the fact that their marriage was childless, but sitting by Neil's sick-bed, not knowing in that first perilous week if he was going to live or die, she had grown to care for him.

She had nursed him back to life — with some help from Mistress Cochrane, she acknowledged briefly — and she didn't want anyone to take him away from her now. She was quite certain, having spoken to the neighbour, Mistress Bothwell, that Ewan Lindsay would not be in a fit state to care for a delicate lad like Neil for a very long time.

In fact, Mistress Bothwell and Sarah had already decided between them that it would be best for the children to make their home permanently at Carriagehill. But that was one of the many domestic decisions that would be kept from Fergus.

As for Rowena — Sarah looked forward to having a little girl to dress and take about in the carriage. It would be just like the old happy days when she had her dolls to play with.

Even as she smiled on them both and slipped out of the room again, hearing Rowena's stumbling reading re-commence as soon as the door closed, Sarah was trying to decide whether pale green or deep blue would suit that red hair best. Or perhaps a soft yellow? She would take the carriage to the Cross the next day and consult her dress-maker, Mistress Gilroy.

Her thoughts turned to Kerr Fraser, who had stumbled out of the gates of the canal basin on that terrible day, carrying Neil Lindsay under one arm and dragging Rowena, screaming and fighting to get back to her parents, with his free hand. It was purely by chance that the Bain carriage had been passing when the uproar began, and had stopped to find out what was happening.

'Take them—' Kerr had said, thrusting the two children into Sarah's arms. 'Take them and get them out of here, for the love of God!'

And without another word, dripping wet and white-faced, he had turned about and plunged back into the screaming, milling, sobbing mass of humanity in and around the basin.

Every day since then, Mistress Cochrane told her, he had presented himself at the back door of the house to ask after the children's welfare.

She herself had seen him leaving after one such visit. She had nodded from the carriage window as the young man stepped to one side of the drive. Always quick to assess a man's qualities, she noted in one glance that he was tall, pleasingly broad-shouldered, with an open square face and honest grey eyes below a tumble of fair hair.

He came of a good Paisley family: indeed, Sarah could recall her mother entertaining the boy's parents in the days before Colin Fraser, a town councillor, fell from grace. Now his widow, Alison, ran a sweet-shop and Kerr, her elder son, worked in Watson and Bain's threadmill.

Yes, Sarah thought as she lifted her skirt delicately and began to descend the staircase, she must see to it that Kerr Fraser was rewarded for having brought her new family — and himself — to her notice.

III

Eighteen-eleven arrived. January and February came and went, and Sarah's replies to Rowena's persistent questions about her father became brief and exasperated.

'He's still not able to think of having you back home. In any case, girl, how can a man on his own look after two children?'

'I can see to the house. I helped mo — mother when Neil was ill. I know what to do.' It was almost impossible to think of her mother, let alone mention her, without crying. Rowena was determined not to cry. It would only give Mistress Bain good reason to repeat that she was too young to look after a house and a delicate child like Neil.

Sure enough, he was brought into Sarah's argument. 'And there's your brother to think of. You heard the physician say we must be careful all through the winter in case the pneumonia comes back, didn't you?' Then she asked plaintively, in the little-girl voice that made Rowena squirm, 'Don't you like it here?'

There was no denying that the Bains were kind and their

home was a palace compared to the house in Common Loan. But Rowena ached for the two familiar rooms and the sound of her father whistling along the street as he returned from the manufactory each night.

Neil, who had wept in Sarah's arms for his mother once he was well enough to learn what had happened, had then dried his tears and settled down happily enough with the toys that had been bought for him.

He was quite prepared to call the Bains 'Aunt Sarah' and 'Uncle Fergus', but the word stuck in Rowena's throat. Mister Bain was her father's employer and Mistress Bain a grand lady. They were no kin to the Lindsay family and it seemed wrong to pretend that they were. She had noticed that Mister Bain looked uncomfortable each time Neil addressed him as 'Uncle Fergus', and deduced that he, too, felt that there was something amiss with the familiarity.

'Folk should bide where they belong,' she said to Ibby, the girl who had been hired as nursery maid.

Ibby sniffed, scrubbed her snub nose with the back of one rough hand, and looked longingly round the room that had been set aside as a day nursery. Her hair had escaped from under her cap and hung about her bony red face in lank strands.

'I'd sooner live here than at home in one room with everyone else,' she said flatly.

'Even if it meant leaving your family?'

The girl screwed up her little brown eyes in thought, then said, 'Aye.'

'But you know you're safe enough, so it's all right for you to—' Rowena began, then stopped as Mistress Cochrane's birdlike cough was heard from the hallway.

Ibby hurled herself under the table and began polishing its legs, hissing, 'I'll get the sharp edge of her tongue if you keep me from my work, Mistress Rowena!'

'Don't call me Mist—' Rowena gave up for the second time as the door opened.

'The carriage is at the door, lassie,' the housekeeper told her crisply, 'Don't keep Mistress Bain waiting.'

It was a mild day, so Neil had been given permission to take some fresh air. Glowing with pleasure at the unexpected outing, he was waiting in the phaeton with their benefactress to take Rowena to Mistress Gilroy's dress-making and millinery establishment in the High Street.

As the neat carriage bowled down into Causewayside Street and then up St Mirren's Street to the dressmaker's shop on the old bridge over the river Neil beamed on all and sundry, while Rowena slid down in her seat and kept her eyes on the floor in a panic of embarrassment in case the people who saw her thought she was putting on airs and graces.

'Sit up, child, do! And stop squinting your eyes like that, you'll give yourself lines like an old woman!' Sarah scolded.

She herself was in her element as she left Neil in the coachman's charge and swept into the little shop with her new ward trailing behind her.

Rowena was measured and talked over like a prize cow in a show-ring. Mistress Gilroy described her red hair as 'auburn', and enthused over her long-lashed brown eyes and fair skin; Sarah, elegant in a pale blue coat trimmed with fur and with a huge matching fur muff, pointed out somewhat coolly that if the wind changed Rowena's face would be stuck in a perpetual glare.

Rowena decided that she would retain the glare whether the wind changed or not. She thought of home, and a lump that had by now become familiar grew in her throat.

At last a frightening number of dresses and petticoats and bonnets had been decided on and ordered, and they were free to go back to the house.

'That'll do to be going on with,' Sarah said with satisfaction as the horses clopped back along Causewayside Street.

'There's too many — I'll have nowhere to keep them when I go back home!'

Neil, oblivious to the conversation, peered from the window, bright spots of colour in his cheeks as he surveyed Paisley from this new, exhilarating angle.

Sarah's pretty mouth tightened. 'Rowena, you're surely old enough to realise that it wouldn't be fair to your father to land him with two children just now.'

'I know how to look after—'

'You've said that before. And as I've told you before, that's a matter of opinion. Make up your mind to it,' Sarah said bracingly, 'You'll not be going back to Common Loan for a good while – if at all.'

She didn't even notice the look of startled horror on Rowena's face, for she had just realised that the carriage was passing her milliner's shop.

'Stop, William! Children, wait here until I come back,' she instructed as she was assisted from the carriage. 'William, you might as well go to the vintner's and enquire whether the claret Mister Bain ordered has arrived yet.'

The coachman ducked his head dutifully and went off along the street. Sarah disappeared into the milliner's just as Rowena realised that they had stopped opposite Common Loan.

'Look, Neil – we're nearly home!' She felt her heart flutter with excitement.

The thought of running away from the Bain house and going back to her father had occurred to her before, but had been dismissed because she wouldn't leave without Neil. She couldn't risk taking him out into the cold winter air and bringing on a recurrence of the frightening illness that had almost taken him from her after the canal disaster.

But now he was with her, and the temptation was overwhelming.

'Come on – we'll go and see how father is.'

Neil looked at her doubtfully. 'But Aunt Sarah said—' he began.

'We'll be back before she is,' Rowena lied. 'Come on, Neil!'

Without stopping to think about it she opened the carriage door and slipped down onto the busy footpath. Neil, after a moment's hesitation, followed. Scampering across the road, dodging the wheeled traffic, they gained the opposite footpath and turned the corner.

Unlike many of their contemporaries who were content to live in rented accommodation, Ewan Lindsay and his wife had scraped together enough money to buy a ground floor house in a two-storey building in Common Loan. It was small, but it was sufficient. Later, as Ewan prospered and the children grew, they planned to move into something better.

The door to the house led off a communal passageway;

Mistress Bothwell, a widowed lady with no children of her own, had the apartment opposite, and a stairway at the rear of the close led to two other houses on the upper floor. A small yard at the back was divided among the tenants. Morag Lindsay had taken great pride in her tiny, well-tended vegetable patch.

The door was on the latch; Rowena only had to push it, and they were inside. At last, they were home.

'Father?'

There was no reply to her tentative call. The door opened straight into the kitchen, which was at the front of the house. A short passageway from the kitchen led to the small bedroom the children had shared. Ewan and Morag had slept in the box bed in the kitchen.

'I want to go back to the carriage,' Neil said uneasily, with an invalid's petulant whine. She caught his hand and held it tightly.

'No — we've come home. We're going to stay with father now!'

Despite her firm words a prickle of fear ran down her spine as the silence circled them like an unfriendly dog. For almost four months, while she waited in the Bain house for her father to come striding up the drive to fetch them, she had kept memories of home alive in her heart. But this cheerless room with its fine patina of dust over once-shining furniture, its faint smell of damp where there had been the aroma of baking, its hush where there had been chatter and laughter and her mother's voice singing lullabies and ballads and funny songs — this wasn't home.

Someone sighed. Neil, thoroughly unnerved, gave an animal-like whimper and the breath almost stopped in Rowena's throat. She forced herself to go forward, towing her brother behind her, round to the front of the high-backed chair that sat by the cold range.

'Father!' Her voice shook with relief.

Ewan Lindsay, huddled in his chair, looked smaller than usual. Even his carroty red hair had lost its glow. His eyes, when they slowly lifted to look at the two of them, were almost blank.

His face had the pallor of one who never went out into the fresh air, and there were lines furrowed into it that Rowena had not seen before; deep, harsh grooves angling down from the corners of his wide mouth.

'It's us, father. We've come home.'

He reached out a hand, but let it drop to his knee again before she could take it.

'It's good of you to call.' His voice was thick with disuse. His head sagged again to his chest and she crouched before the chair so that she could look up into his face.

'Why didn't you come to bring us home? Why didn't you come to see Neil when he was so ill?'

Ewan frowned as though her questions were flies buzzing round his head.

'I've been − I've had things to see to − think about. Morag − Morag—'

The name seemed to dissolve in his mouth. To her horror Rowena saw tears fill his eyes and start to spill down his pale face. Her own ready tears gathered, and were blinked away.

'Come away, Rowena—' Neil's voice was high and tremulous.

'Sit down!' She pushed him into a chair opposite Ewan, looked about the room.

'Now − we need a good fire for a start, and I'll have to give the place a right clean up—' The taste of her mother's brisk words on her own lips gave her strength. 'I'll have to set to and turn it out, I can see that. But first we'd best have some hot tea. And I'll make scones—'

She lifted the cover on the once-gleaming range, seized a poker and stirred the dully glowing ashes within. She put in more coal and swung the kettle over the range to heat water, trying to recall how her mother had baked scones.

Once she got the room warmed up and got some food inside her menfolk they would feel happier. Then the three of them could settle down and plan their future.

'I want to go home,' Neil said.

'You are home!' She rounded on him fiercely.

His mouth squared. He put his hands on the wooden arms of the chair, ready to push himself to his feet, his blue eyes watching her warily. 'I want to go home to Carriagehill.'

'No!'

He began to cough, but she heartlessly paid no heed. She could tell when Neil was playing the invalid.

Now tears were rolling down Ewan's face. Pretending that she hadn't noticed them either, Rowena lifted the big heavy griddle from its hook on the wall, put it on the range, opened the cupboard door, and found to her dismay that the flour crock, always filled and ready for use in the past, was empty.

As she stared into its depths, a voice asked from the doorway, 'What are you doing in this house?'

Mistress Bothwell stood there, wearing her usual black silk dress, her face hostile.

'For all the world like a crow that's fallen out of a tree!' Rowena suddenly recalled her mother's mischievous remark about their neighbour, and her father's laughter. But he wasn't laughing now.

'We've come home. I'm going to look after them both now.' She got to her feet and faced the woman, who gave that derisive sniff Rowena remembered so well.

'You? How could a bairn like you look after a house! Is Mistress Bain wandered, letting the pair of you come back here?' Then, as she glanced from Rowena to Neil, now standing wretchedly in the middle of the room, her eyes narrowed. 'Does she know where you are?'

'It's not her business!' And it's not yours, Rowena wanted to add, but dared not.

The woman moved further into the room and stood by Ewan's chair. 'That's a fine way to speak of the lady who took you and your brother in when you were left motherless. Go back to her house this instant, lassie.'

'We're staying with our father!'

'I don't want to!' Neil wailed treacherously, ignoring the glare she gave him. 'I want to go back to Carriagehill. I don't feel well!'

Mistress Bothwell's eyes glittered. 'Can you not see what you're doing to the boy — and to your father as well? The man's sick with grieving; he doesn't want children under his feet at a time like this!'

The words lashed at Rowena so hard she could almost feel them as weals marking her soft skin. She was suddenly demoralised as she realised that she was only a child, with no rights whatsoever and no way of fighting the grown-up conspiracy that kept what was left of her family apart.

'You can't tell me what to do — you're not my mother!' Her voice shook despite her efforts to steady it. Mistress Bothwell's stern face darkened.

'You're a wicked, ungrateful lassie! If I had been your mother you'd know better how to mind your manners — you'd not be worrying the life out of your father and those that have tried to care for you in their Christian goodness and charity!' Mistress Bothwell came to lean over her, her black-clad body cutting Rowena off from her father, her voice low. 'If I'd been your mother there'd have been no sinful gallivanting in canal boats, flouting the good Lord and bringing down a cruel judgment—'

The tears Rowena had been fighting back since she first saw her father broke free under the tirade, and the room shimmered about her.

Widow Bothwell left her and went to Ewan, her long, strong fingers settling possessively on his shoulder.

'Get back to Mistress Bain and pray to the Lord to make you good and ease your father's suffering. Go along, now, and take your brother with you!'

'I won't!'

'Little children have been cast into the fires of Hell for less impudence than that, Rowena Lindsay!' Mistress Bothwell snapped, then her face was suddenly, grotesquely lit with a grim smile of triumph.

'Neil!'

The scent of violets filled the little room as Sarah Bain swept past Rowena to gather Neil into her arms. Then, and only then, did she turn to face his sister.

'What d'you think you're doing, bringing him here when he's not long been snatched from death's very door?'

'I—' The words she wanted to speak died in her throat as she looked at the two women, from different worlds but united in their condemnation of wicked, ungrateful Rowena Lindsay.

The Widow Bothwell's lips pursed with gratification. 'I think it would be best if you took them away, Mistress Bain.'

'Indeed.' Sarah took a firmer grip on Neil's hand. 'Come along, Rowena—'

'Father?'

He looked up, his empty eyes moving from his son to his

daughter. For a moment she thought that he was going to intervene, then 'Leave me be,' he said quietly; whether to her, or to the world in general, she didn't know. And he looked down again at his idle hands.

'You see? Your father doesn't want you,' said Sarah with unintentional cruelty. 'Now come along—'

Numbly, Rowena allowed herself to be led out of the house, along the footpath, and across the road to where the carriage waited. But when the coachman was about to help her into it she shook her head, backing away from him.

'I want to walk back.'

Sarah, already seated, Neil held protectively against her, sighed in exasperation. 'Walk — on your own? How can you be trusted to — be careful, you clumsy child!'

The warning came too late. Rowena had already backed into someone who grunted as her head collided with his ribs. She looked up, into a square, strong, familiar face.

'It's Kerr Fraser, isn't it?' Sarah was already asking.

'Your servant, ma'am.'

She inclined her bonneted head graciously, then her voice switched from honey to ice as she turned back to her tiresome ward. 'Rowena, d'you hear me?'

'I'm not going in the carriage!' She would have taken to her heels if Kerr's hand hadn't been on her shoulder.

'And you're not going to be allowed to walk back by yourself!'

'Kerr could walk with me. Couldn't you?'

Surprise and embarrassment chased each other across his face. 'I — I must call in at my mother's shop first, but after that, if you want—'

'Well—' Sarah hesitated, then gave him one of her most charming smiles. 'I'd be most obliged, Mister Fraser. William, drive on—'

As the wheels started to turn Neil looked guiltily, apologetically, down at his sister. She tried to summon up a fierce face, but to her horror the emotional drama of the past hour had beaten her, and hot tears came back to her eyes. She turned away so that he couldn't see her weakness.

'I'm not going back,' she told Kerr as the carriage moved away. 'I'm not — I'm not!' The tears began to spill down her cheeks.

He looked down at her in a quandary, then 'We'll see what my mother says,' he said. 'Will that content you?'

Numbly, she nodded and let him lead her, still weeping, to the building where his mother had turned the front room of her ground-floor house into a small confectionery.

The rear door in the outside passageway led directly into a little kitchen, where Kerr put Rowena into a big chair by the fire.

'Wait there. I'll fetch my mother.'

He went through an inner door and she was alone in a room very like the sort of kitchen her own mother had ruled over in the happy days before the *Countess of Eglinton* heeled over in the canal basin.

The grate had been thoroughly black-leaded, the floor was freshly swept and the wooden dresser shone. Incongruously, one wall was dominated by a huge framed painting of a handsome man in a black coat over a white ruffled shirt; there was a great gold chain decorated with seals across the front of the shirt.

The portrait excited her curiosity at once. It was completely out of place in this cosy little kitchen.

The door that had closed behind Kerr opened, and a gentle voice asked, 'Rowena?'

'Y – yes, ma – ma'am—' She got to her feet, hiccuping as she tried to subdue her sobs.

The woman by the door was over-thin. Soft grey hair framed a pleasant, tired face; her eyes, like her son's, were grey. At that moment, as she surveyed the tear-stained child before her, they were compassionate.

'Oh – you poor wee thing!' said Mistress Fraser, and came across the room to scoop Rowena onto her lap. 'Poor wee pet!'

It was impossible to be brave under such circumstances – and it was such a relief to be able to go back to babyhood and nestle in the safety of someone's arms.

Rowena was finally free to weep for her mother and for what her father had become, to sob out her hidden fears over Neil's illness, her loneliness in the big house on Carriagehill, her resentment at being taken over as if she was a puppy instead of a human being.

Bit by bit the story came out, while Mistress Fraser rocked her and made soothing noises.

'My m — mother wasn't s — sinful. She wasn't being bad. She ju — just wanted to on the c — canal. And Mistress B — Bothwell said I was—'

'Aye, you've already told me what she said.' Alison Fraser had taken Rowena's bonnet off and had tidied her hair while she listened. Now she put her gently aside and got to her feet. 'Sit down there, now, and I'll wash the tear-stains from your wee face.'

She fetched a wet cloth and cleaned Rowena up, talking all the while.

'You have to try to understand, Rowena, that your father's missing your mother dearly, but in a different way from you. You must give him time to come back to himself.'

'But why should Mistress Bothwell think it was a sin to go on the canal boat?'

Alison sighed. 'Och, some folk think that any sort of pleasure's sinful. They feel that if the Lord had meant us to travel by water He'd have shaped us like herring.'

The thought made Rowena give a hiccuping giggle.

'You see? There's a smile in everything.' Alison put the wash-cloth aside and took both Rowena's hands in a safe, warm grip. 'You're a good brave girl, but you're truly not old enough to take on the responsibility of caring for your father and your brother — not just yet.'

'When?'

'Well now, it could take a few years. You must be patient, for everyone's sake. Mistress Bain's good to you, is she not?'

'Yes, but — it's not home. It's not like this place—' She looked round the cosy room, similar to the kitchen in Common Loan as she had known it, and a thought suddenly exploded in her head.

'Can Neil and me not stay here, with you instead?'

Alison's eyes widened. 'Oh — lassie, I've already got my own sons—'

'I could help in the shop and clean the house—' the words hurried from Rowena. 'Me and Neil wouldn't take up much room. I'm strong — I could do whatever you wanted me to do!'

Mistress Fraser's grey eyes were troubled. 'Rowena—'

'Please!'

'Mother, you're wanted in the shop.'

Neither of them had heard the door to the front room opening. Kerr Fraser stood there, his square face expressionless. 'And it's time she was home. I'll take her back to Carriagehill.'

Rowena held tight to the arms of the chair, glaring at this youth who had led her to Paradise and was now trying to take her away from it again.

Alison Fraser straightened, began to speak, then met her son's eye and stopped. Her hand cupped Rowena's uplifted face gently, her eyes were kind as she said 'Visit us again, lassie, any time you want.'

'On you go to the shop. I'll see to her.' Kerr stepped aside to let her pass, then he closed the door and advanced across the floor to where Rowena huddled in the chair. He stood over her, his jaw set firmly.

'Don't you start thinking you'll find a haven here, Rowena Lindsay,' he said. 'Because you won't!'

IV

'Your mother said—'

'I'm not bothered about what she said,' Kerr interrupted. 'If she'd her way of it she'd take in every motherless bairn in the town, and the Lord knows there's little enough to keep the three of us as it is, what with—'

He stopped abruptly, glanced up at the big portrait. 'No use trying to explain anything to a wee lassie like you. I'm taking you back to Mistress Bain now, as I promised.'

She had the sense to see that there was no defying him. Slowly she got down off the chair and stood before him, fists clenched.

'I hate you, Kerr Fraser!'

He reached down from his great height and took her shoulders in his hands, shaking her gently but firmly. 'No you don't. Listen to me – you've got to go back, and you've got to learn that there's no easy way out for the likes of us. Come on now, your brother's waiting.'

At the door to the close he held out his hand. 'Here – some of my mother's sweeties for you.'

She wanted to refuse, but she daren't invite his anger. So she accepted the neatly wrapped screw of paper and put it into her skirt pocket.

At first he strode along Causewayside Street ahead of her and she had to run in a vain attempt to keep up with him. Then, realising that she wasn't by his side, he stopped and looked back to where she trotted, breathless, several yards behind.

To her surprise he held out a large hand. She took it shyly, and his fingers closed about hers.

Past shops and houses they went, then the buildings gave way to a stretch of road bordered by fields before they reached the outer limits of the town where the wealthier residents lived.

In this era when women throughout the country were proud to boast at least one colourful Paisley shawl in their wardrobes, the rich townspeople were mainly shawl manufacturers.

Now there were fewer pedestrians to dodge round and it was easier for Rowena to keep up with Kerr's long strides. But she let her hand lie in his, for his clasp gave her some comfort.

He swung into the Bain driveway between open wrought-iron gates and marched up the front steps to the wide, imposing door, set in an elegantly-carved wooden casing and with a half-moon glass window above it. It opened as he raised his hand to the polished brass knocker, and Sarah Bain herself stood there, smiling on them both.

'Here you are at last, Rowena. Come in, Mister Fraser.'

She swept the two of them into the square entrance hall, and Kerr removed his three-cornered hat – the same one, Rowena suddenly realised, that Neil had knocked off that day at the canal. Her mouth trembled at the memory, and she counter-acted the weakness by digging her nails into the palms of her hands.

'Neil's waiting upstairs, Rowena. He refused to eat anything until you got home.' Sarah turned to Kerr. 'You'll take a glass of Madeira, Mister Fraser?'

He bobbed his head in a bow that was brief, but without

clumsiness or discourtesy. 'Thank you, Mistress Bain, but I've to get back to the mill now.'

'You shall — in just five short minutes.' There was a coquettish note in Sarah's voice as she put a white hand on his arm and turned him towards the drawing-room door. 'You must let me show my gratitude — our gratitude.'

Rowen's legs ached after trotting all the way from Gordon's Lane. The wide staircase, curving gracefully to the upper floors, looked as steep as a mountain. Slowly, holding onto the carved balustrade, she started the climb. On the third tread she stopped and looked back. Sarah's hand was on the sleeve of Kerr's jacket in a way that reminded Rowena of Mistress Bothwell's possessive hand on her father's arm.

She drew him through the double doors and into the big room, much like a spider triumphantly carrying a captive fly to the corner of its web. Then she turned and closed the doors, a small smile playing about her lips.

Rowena, left to her own devices, trudged on up the staircase.

When she opened the door of the room that Sarah called the day nursery Neil launched himself from the carpet, where he had been playing with some new toy soldiers.

Two spots of colour glowed in his pale face and his eyes glittered with unshed tears. His fists gripped the lapels of her jacket and he shook her so hard that she staggered, taken unawares, and her bonneted head rebounded painfully off the doorframe.

'You wouldn't come back with me!' he shrieked. 'You went away and left me and I didn't know where you were—!'

'Neil—' She had no time to say any more. For all his year's seniority he was only an inch taller than she was, and not much heavier, but the unexpectedness of his attack was too much for her tired legs.

Locked together, brother and sister crashed to the floor, Neil sobbing and trying to pummel her and hold her at the same time, Rowena defending herself as best she could.

'Mistress Rowena! Master Neil!' Ibby, easing her way in with a loaded tray from the kitchen, managed to avoid their kicking legs long enough to put the tray safely on the table. Then she delved into the struggle and separated them.

'Is this any way to behave? D'you want to get me into trouble?'

'She went away and left me!' Neil howled.

'I didn't! You could've come with me!' Rowena, scrambling to her feet now that the nursery maid had pulled him off her, took time to look at his trembling mouth, his frightened eyes. She recalled that Neil, for all his seniority, wasn't as strong and healthy as she was. She realised that the change in their father had terrified him and that she had deserted him just when he needed all the reassurance he could get. A wave of love and remorse swept over her.

'I'm sorry, Neil. Look—' She pulled the packet Kerr Fraser had given her from her pocket and held it out. 'I got some sweets for you.'

Sniffing, rubbing the tears from his cheeks with his other hand, he reached out and claimed the screw of paper.

'You can just put these by till later,' Ibby ordered, busying herself about the table. 'Your dinner's been keeping hot on the kitchen range for the past hour or more. Sit up and eat it and let me get on with my work.'

Although it had begun to dry up the dish of fresh-caught cod, brought up the River Cart that morning by boat, cooked in a parsley sauce and served with potatoes, was appetising. Rowena discovered that she was starving, and began to shovel food into her mouth with no regard for good table manners.

She caught Neil's eye and gave him a tentative smile. He began to smile back, stopped himself in time, and buried his face in a mug of weak tea. Above the rim of the mug his silky black eyebrows were knotted fiercely.

'Neil—' she said with sudden inspiration. 'Did you ever think that if God meant folk to travel by water He'd have shaped us like herrings?'

The eyebrows unravelled and shot up in two astonished question marks. Then Neil spluttered tea all over the table and Ibby's skirt. The mug thumped down onto the once-spotless cloth as he broke into a bellow of mirth.

Rowena joined in, rocking herself back and forth in her chair until the legs thumped on the polished floor.

'Mistress Rowena!' said Ibby, scandalised, 'That's blasphemy!

And look at the table — look at my skirt! I swear I don't know what to do with you two! I'm fair affronted!'

Her mouth was a shocked circle in her red face, but Rowena and Neil paid no attention. Their laughter mingled and rose to the high ceiling, beating against the windows, uniting to defy the world outside.

*

Fergus Bain smiled to himself as he came in through the front door and heard the children's laughter echoing from the upper floor. It was good for him, and for Sarah, to have young people about the house, he thought indulgently.

He normally went into his library when he came home from the mill, but today, hearing the laughter, he suddenly wanted to be with his wife. Perhaps they would go together to the nursery; it was time he got to know the children.

As he went in Sarah jumped up from a deep, comfortable sofa that stood facing the fireplace, with its back to the double doors. Her face was becomingly flushed; her brows were crescents of surprise when she saw her husband.

'Fergus! What are you doing home so early?'

'I've surely earned the right to come home when I please,' he said mildly, then his own brows climbed as a fine-looking young man rose from the sofa to face him.

'So — it's yourself, Kerr?'

Fergus would have found it hard to put even a surname to most of the two or three hundred souls who worked in the mill, but the son of a former, though fallen, town official was different. Even so, he was surprised to find the lad being entertained in his drawing-room.

'Kerr brought Rowena home, and I invited him to take a glass of Madeira,' Sarah said quickly. Her husband's eyes moved to the youth's empty hands, and she flushed.

'He's just arrived.'

'Sit down, lad, and let me act upon my wife's invitation.'

Pouring the wine into fine crystal glasses, he decided that he liked the boy's manner; respectful, without being subordinate.

When he turned, it was to see that Sarah had seated herself again on the sofa, but Kerr had moved to a straight-backed chair. He himself, when he had given his wife's guest his glass, took up his favourite position before the fireplace.

'You're not needed at the mill today?'

Kerr's grey eyes met his without evasion. 'I was there all night. We've been having trouble with one of the carding machines. The manager said I could take a few hours off today.'

'How's your mother?'

'Very well, Mister Bain. She has to work hard, though.'

'Aye, I can believe it. There are two younger than you at home, are there not?'

The boy's face clouded momentarily, like a clear sky swept by a sudden squall. 'Only my brother Philip. Marion died of the consumption last year.'

'I'm sorry. I hadn't realised—' Fergus said awkwardly. He looked to his wife for assistance, but Sarah was silent, hands clasped in her lap, pursed lips betraying her displeasure at his unexpected return.

He cleared his throat and changed the subject. 'And how d'you find your work at the mill?'

Kerr's face lit up. 'I like tending the machinery.'

Now that the talk had moved to something he understood, Fergus was on comfortable ground. He was sorry when Kerr put down his glass, still half-full, and excused himself.

'I hope you'll visit with me again, Mister Fraser,' Sarah said sweetly as he bowed with a certain natural grace over her hand. 'You must dine with us one evening.'

'I doubt if the boy would be comfortable at our dinner table,' Fergus said when they were alone.

'I see no reason why.' His wife's voice was tart.

'D'you ever call on his mother?'

'How can I, now that she's a shopkeeper?'

'So now she's not good enough for Mistress Sarah Bain. And yet—' there was an edge now to Fergus's voice '—you want to invite her son, who's only a machine-minder, to dine at your table?'

As Sarah began to flounce angrily towards the door, he added, 'Isn't he somewhat young for you, my dear?'

She whirled to face him. 'What d'you mean by that?'

'I've been keeping an eye on Kerr Fraser. He's a good worker and he'll do well for himself by his own efforts. Leave him be, Sarah,' said Fergus, and walked out, leaving his wife trembling with fury in the middle of her fine drawing-room.

The next day he made arrangements for Kerr Fraser to go on the road, learning how to sell Watson and Bain's thread throughout the length and breadth of Great Britain.

*

Rowena knew nothing of Kerr's departure until Ibby happened to mention it casually. Then the little maid squeaked as Rowena seized her shoulders.

'What did you say?'

Ibby pulled herself free. 'Only that Kerr's been set to travelling for the mill—'

'When?'

'He's leaving today, on the five o'clock coach to Glasgow — where are you going?'

'Rowena, where are you going?' Sarah Bain wanted to know as her foster-daughter sped down the staircase and through the hall as though the fiends of Hell were after her.

'Out,' said Rowena shortly, intent on gaining the front door.

'But my dear child, you can't—'

'I'll not be long. I've to see a friend—' She tossed the words over her shoulder as she ran out of the house, along the short drive, through the gates, and off along the road to Paisley.

The stage-coaches to Glasgow left from Waingaitend. To get there Rowena had to run the length of Causewayside Street then up St Mirren Street and across the High Street.

By the time she reached the coach and the small knot of people clustered about it she was out of breath but triumphant, for she was in time to see Kerr leave for his new life.

He was already aboard the cumbersome vehicle, leaning down to talk to his mother and his younger brother Philip, who had just started his weaving apprenticeship. Suddenly shy and reluctant to break in on the family's farewells, Rowena loitered on the fringe of the crowd, gathering her breath and hoping that Kerr might look up and see her.

The final passenger was hauled aboard and the coachman took his seat and gathered up the reins. As the coach began to move Kerr looked up, his eyes raking the crowd as though searching for someone. Rowena lifted her hand in the beginnings of a wave, then lowered it, feeling foolish, as his gaze brushed past her and moved on.

It fixed on a spot just behind her. His face lit up and he raised a hand in brief salute, then the coach was on the move, and Rowena lost sight of him.

She turned and saw a girl behind her, flourishing a kerchief at the coach. A lovely girl of about Kerr's age, with striking violet eyes. A girl with black curls framing a face of gypsy-like vitality.

The crowd began to break up. Alison Fraser, Philip by her side, began to walk slowly homewards without noticing Rowena.

The unknown girl was also turning away when a lad stopped her and spoke to her, a hand on her arm. She laughed up into his face and the two of them began to walk together towards the Cross.

It was time for Rowena to scurry home to face the scolding that was almost certainly waiting for her. As she went, she felt that once again she had suffered a loss.

She scarcely knew Kerr Fraser, but he had saved her life, and he had introduced her to the safe haven behind the sweet shop.

Somehow, Paisley wouldn't be the same place without him in it.

V

The frilled pantalettes soared through the air, legs waving plaintively as they went. They caught for a moment on a painting of kittens playing with a ball then fell to the floor.

'Leave them—' Rowena instructed as Ibby scurried across the bedroom to retrieve the rejected underwear.

'But Mi — but Rowena!' the maid wailed. 'If Mistress Cochrane sees them—'

'Then take them away, out of my sight. Give them to your wee sister. I was thirteen years old yesterday and I will not wear those childish clothes one moment longer!'

It sometimes occurred to Ibby's confused mind that almost every sentence she spoke to her young charge began with 'But'.

'But what else will you wear, if not your pantalettes?'

'These.' Rowena triumphantly rummaged beneath her pillow then held out a pair of green silk stockings. 'I bought them in the town yesterday.'

She sat on a low stool and began to draw the stockings over her long legs, adding, as the maidservant continued to wring her hands and utter small clucks of distress, 'And if you or Mistress Cochrane or Mistress Bain dare to say a word against them I'll buy scarlet woollen hose instead. Or mebbe even striped ones!'

Ibby, stuffing the rejected pantaloons into the front of her big loose apron so that the housekeeper wouldn't see them, had the wit to hold her tongue.

Satisfied with the stockings, Rowena stepped into her petticoat and then her best sprigged muslin dress with its delicate pastel pattern scattered over a white background. The sleeves were demurely long and frilled at the wrists; the collar had been high when Sarah Bain first had the dress made for her, but

Rowena had recently taken her needle to it, lowering the neck-line and edging it with a crisp ruffle of white lace.

She nodded at herself in the mirror and smoothed the thin material over her hips. Then she tied a small-brimmed bonnet over the luxuriously thick hair that had deepened in the four years since the canal boat disaster from red to glossy auburn.

For a wonder, Neil was at home and in his bedroom when she put her head round the door of the old night nursery. Sarah had decided that as he was now a student at the Grammar School he required plenty of space for studying, so his was the larger room of the two, a big, airy apartment with a fine view of the garden. The former day nursery had become Rowena's bedroom. Her window looked out at the side of the house, onto high thick shrubbery edging the Bains' property.

'Coming with me, Neil?' She tried hard not to sound too eager for his company. 'I'm going to see father.'

'Why?' he asked without bothering to raise his head from the pack of cards he was shuffling through long flexible fingers.

She advanced into the room. 'You know fine I visit him now and then.'

'Why?' Neil asked again, and this time he looked up. Now fourteen years of age, he had outgrown the croup and asthma that had come close to killing him on more than one occasion. In the past year he had grown rapidly, and was now a good head taller than his sister. He was naturally pale-skinned and this, together with his black silky hair, dark eyebrows, clear blue eyes and high cheekbones, made him a good-looking youth. Those looks could often be marred by the old square-mouthed petu-lant grimace he had retained from childhood.

'Does he welcome you? Is he pleased to see you? Does he watch for you coming?' Without waiting for an answer he swept on angrily, 'When are you going to see that you might as well forget about him the way he's forgotten about us?'

'He's not! He's not forgotten us!'

'When did he ever come up to this house to see us — even to find out if we were still alive?'

The cards sprayed to the floor in a pattern of black and white and red as he tossed them down impatiently. 'It's been five years, nearly! How can you go on pretending that we matter to him? No, I'm not going to see him. Not today, not ever!'

He pushed his chair aside and went to stare from the window, his back to her. 'I've got another mother now, and so have you. A father too, if it comes to that. And we've a better life here than we'd have had with him. Keep away from the past, Rowena, it can only harm you!'

Hurt was a hot flood that almost showed itself in tears. Never, never, would she let Sarah and Fergus Bain, for all their kindness, take the place of the parents who had brought her into the world. She stood undecided for a moment then left him, realising that nothing she said or did would change Neil's attitude towards the man who had left them to be brought up by people who were no kin to them.

Her naturally buoyant spirits returned as she walked down the road, revelling in the freedom of movement the new stockings gave her. A lovely June day was drawing to its close, and the air was still warm, sensually heavy with the day's sun.

At the crossroads where Gordon's Loan led off to her right and Common Loan to her left she stopped, buffeted by the people hurrying past. Should she visit her father first, or Mistress Fraser?

She turned towards her old home, then perversely changed her mind and skipped across busy Causewayside Street and along Gordon's Loan.

The sweet-shop was situated in a row of sturdy low stone-built houses that fronted the south-east side of the lane. Behind their back yards ran the Espedair Burn and above the slate roofs, as she waited to let a cart laden with cloth lumber by before crossing the lane, Rowena could see the grassy dome of Saucel Hill.

It was said that the hill was the tomb of two brothers, plague sufferers who had taken shelter in a cave there hundreds of years before. Monks from the great Abbey on the opposite bank of the river had fed the sick men and, when they died, had blocked up the cave entrance with rocks to keep the dread disease from escaping. Today, the Abbey was a ruin and the hill, fresh and green, belied its sinister past — but even so, the townspeople never went too close to its great bulk after dark, for fear the poor souls trapped deep within tried to escape and walk the night.

The shop bell jangled as she went in. The small room, shelves packed with row upon row of crocks, was empty.

'It's only me—' she called cheerfully, and went through the door that led to the kitchen beyond.

The air was fragrant with the rich smell of the freshly made toffee Alison was pouring into trays from a large pan. She looked up and her tired face creased in a warm smile.

'Come away in, lass.'

With the ease of one at home in her surroundings Rowena picked up a cloth to protect her hands and lifted the second pan, a fine perspiration breaking out on her brow as heat rose up and surrounded her. Carefully, she began to pour out the thick dark mixture.

Serenity always came over her when she was with Alison Fraser. Remembering the day when Kerr had brought her to this kitchen for the first time, then denied her the right to stay, she wondered if she would have been a better, less rebellious person if she had had her way that day and become one of the Fraser household.

'You're a kind soul.' Alison put her empty container down, eased her back, and then scrubbed at her flushed face with a corner of her apron. 'Times I wish I'd taken on an easier way of earning a living. But I never was all that good with my needle, so I'd not have made much progress as a seamstress or a milliner.' She sank into a chair, motioned to Rowena to sit down as well. 'I'm just thankful that my mother taught me how to make sweets.'

Her face, emerging from the folds of the apron, was suddenly radiant.

'I got a letter from Philip this morning. His very first, since he went to be a soldier!' She took the folded sheet of paper from her apron pocket and thrust it at Rowena. 'I've near read the writing off the page already. Say it out loud, to let me hear how the words sound.'

The clear rounded handwriting could be read with ease. 'Dear Mother,' Alison's younger son had written from the Southern Netherlands several months before: 'I make it my business to acquaint you that I have been in Perfect good Health since I wrote you last thanks be to God — earnestly wishing that these lines may find you all the same.

'I have seen some of my townsmen while here among whom was William Barr who desires to be remembered to his Father and Mother and is to write to them. We are well supplied with very good Provisions and the Army in General was never in Better health and Spirits. I hope that you will be so good as write to me on receipt of this letting me know your situation and that of the Country in General—'

Philip, thought Rowena at this point, was a true son of Paisley, deeply interested in everything that might affect the town's fortunes.

'—and give me word on my Brother Kerr, who last Wrote to me from London. I shall add no more at present but Remain Your Loving and Dutiful Son Philip Fraser.'

She folded the paper carefully and handed it back. 'He's happy enough.'

'And so far travelled!' Alison marvelled. 'Imagine my Philip in a land where they don't even speak the King's English, let alone a good Scots tongue. It seems only yesterday he was no higher than my knee. Pray God he stays safe. But I've no doubt the Duke will look after all his brave lads.'

'Have you had word of Kerr?'

'Not since the last time you were here. I fair miss the two of them.' Alison set to marking the cooling toffee into squares with the blunt side of a knife as she talked. 'The older you get, the harder it is to accept change, Rowena. But life's all crossroads and turnings, isn't it? There's Philip and Kerr both grown and gone, and look at you, a young lady now—' Her eyes twinkled as she indicated the silk stockings. 'And there's your father's marriage—'

'Yes.' Rowena's throat suddenly felt as though it was filled with the soft white fluff that clung to the mill-girls' cloaks as they made their way home after work.

Alison laid down the knife and put a gentle hand on her arm.

'You've still not come round to that, have you, for all that it's been six months now.'

'It's – why did he choose to marry with Mistress Bothwell?' She recalled, with a clarity that made it seem like yesterday, her mother shivering over some gloomy prediction of Mistress

Bothwell's, and her father laughing, kissing his wife, telling her that the Widow Bothwell wasn't to be taken seriously.

'Folk marry for a lot of reasons, lassie. Love, if they're fortunate, or mebbe just for comfort and companionship—'

The bell over the shop door tinkled and Alison automatically put up her hands to tidy her hair before attending to her customers.

'I'll be back in a minute.'

'I must go myself.' Rowena picked up her bonnet as the older woman went out.

As she tied the ribbons beneath her chin she looked up at Colin Fraser's fine portrait, the only memento Alison had of the past. She had heard his story years before from Ibby, who had been raised in Gordon's Loan and knew the Frasers well.

Colin Fraser had been a councillor and property owner until one winter when there had been a scandal over a widow and her two young children who lodged in a wretched dwelling house that he owned. Threatened with eviction, the woman had been forced to pawn everything, including her shoes and the children's bedding, to pay her rent.

Shortly after that she and her children had been found dead from the bitter cold.

The town had rung with the shameful news. Two weeks later, unable to face his fellow-councillors, Colin Fraser killed himself.

It was only then that Alison discovered he had been losing heavily at the gambling tables and borrowing to try to make ends meet. She had given up her fine house and removed her young family to Gordon's Loan, where she had opened the sweet-shop and worked hard, with Kerr's help as soon as he was old enough to go into the threadmill, to pay off her husband's debts. These debts, Rowena understood from Ibby, were not completely cleared yet.

She was still gazing up at the picture when Alison came back into the room.

'There's a look of Kerr — but Kerr has a stronger face.'

Alison came to stand beside her, reaching out to flick an imagined speck of dust from the immaculate frame. 'Aye, he's got great inner strength, has Kerr. He's needed it, poor lad. I wish his way could've been easier. But he'll manage fine.'

A picture flashed into Rowena's mind — Kerr on the stage-coach, his grey eyes passing her, seeking another.

'Has he a sweetheart?'

'I doubt it. His letters are full of nothing but his work and the places he's seen.'

'I mean here, in Paisley.'

Alison carried a bowl of risen dough from the range to the big table. 'There was one he was set to wed if he'd stayed — Eliza Wilson, her name was.'

'He might wed her still.'

'She wasn't the kind who'd wait for any man.' Alison kneaded the dough with practised skill. 'No sooner was he out of Paisley than she upped and went off with someone else. I'm not even sure if she married him first. They were always a shiftless lot, the Wilsons. The rest of the family's scattered to the four winds too. The mother lived in a wee place in Espedair Street, but to the best of my knowledge she never heard from Eliza again. She's dead now, poor soul. It's when I see folk like her,' said Alison thoughtfully, punching and folding the dough, 'I thank the good Lord twice over for my own two.'

VI

Mistress Bothwell — even after six months it was impossible to think of her by any other name — opened the door.

'It's you,' she said flatly, then her black eyes flared as they swooped over her visitor and took in the neat silk-clad ankles.

She glanced up and down the street as though afraid that some passer-by might have noticed them too, then whisked Rowena into the house and shut the door.

The material of her black dress, her iron-grey hair, even her skin seemed to send forth wafts of sanctimony. The cottage carried the stamp of its current mistress; it was spotlessly clean and reeked of carbolic and piety; but even on this sunny day it was chilly.

Ewan sat by the empty range, a newspaper beneath his hand. He glanced up, one finger marking his place, his brow furrowing at the interruption.

'Your daughter's come to call.' His wife took her seat on a wooden chair by the table, picking up her sewing.

Ewan plucked at the pages on his lap. The listlessness that had come over him when his first wife drowned still held him in its grip. It seemed to Rowena that her father had released his hold on life and allowed it to take him wherever it pleased, like a river in spate. He was still store-man at Watson and Bain, where he attended to his duties efficiently enough.

Mistress Bothwell had seen to it that his house was clean and his meals prepared. Ewan had become more and more dependent on her, and although Rowena had railed to Ibby about the marriage, most of the women in the town saw it as both inevitable and sensible, given the way Ewan's widowed neighbour had devoted herself to him.

'You're well, Rowena?'

'Yes, father.'

'And you're behaving yourself?'

'Yes, father.'

'Aye.' He peered at her from beneath shaggy brows then returned with relief to his reading, one finger trailing over the print on the page before him. His lips moved as he read, the dry rustle of his whispering sounding loud in the room's uneasy silence.

In the old days visitors to this kitchen had been made instantly welcome. The fire was poked into a cheerful blaze if the day was the least bit cool, tea was made from the kettle simmering at all times on the hob, scones or oatcakes fresh from the oven were buttered and piled onto plates. But things had changed. The second Mistress Lindsay, welcoming and animated as a dry twig, sat on her chair as though she had no intention of ever moving again, and the well-polished empty kettle on the range glittered as coldly as her eyes.

As ever, it fell to Rowena to fill the silence with words. 'I've been to see Mistress Fraser. She's had word from Philip at last. He's well.'

'She's a poor deserted soul, Alison Fraser.' A sepulchral note came into the woman's harsh voice. 'She's got the look of one not long for this world.'

'She's fine!' Rowena felt an icy finger trailing down her spine. Now she knew what had caused superstitious people once to accuse old women of wishing ill-health.

Her step-mother sniffed. 'And what news of the other lad?'

'Nothing new as yet.'

'He's a son to be proud of, Kerr Fraser,' Ewan said unexpectedly.

'You've a good son too, father. Neil was enquiring after you,' Rowena lied.

'I saw him at the Cross two days past.' Mistress Lindsay's words dripped disapproval. 'Lounging with a crowd of wastrels. Satan finds mischief for hands that lie idle.'

Rowena looked at the clock. The minute hand had scarcely moved since her arrival. She dredged her mind for harmless items of town gossip and delivered them, each one received and underlined by a caustic remark from her step-mother.

Out in the sunshine again ten minutes later, she expelled her breath in a long sigh. These visits cost her a great deal of effort, but she refused to let her step-mother discourage her. Once she stopped visiting Ewan the fragile thread that linked the little family would be broken for ever. For her dead mother's sake, as well as her own, Rowena refused to let that happen.

As she walked up the drive she saw that Sarah's smart little phaeton was waiting before the door. Sarah herself was in the hall, a light shawl about her shoulders.

'Rowena, you look unbecomingly hot and your bonnet ribbons are coming untied.' Her eyes travelled down, seeking more faults, then widened as they reached the slim silk-clad ankles beneath the skirt of Rowena's muslin dress.

'And just what do you think you're wearing? How could you go out looking like that — what must folk think of me?'

'I'm no longer a child, and I'll not dress like one.'

Sarah's lips compressed but she said no more, sweeping past her rebellious charge and out of the door.

*

Sitting upright in the carriage, smoothing her gloves over her hands, Sarah reflected bitterly on the day she had said to Fergus, 'I'll have a wee girl of my own!'

Little had she known then what a strong-willed creature she'd taken under her roof. There had been never a hint of the biddable, pretty little daughter she'd planned to dress and show off like an animated doll.

She realised that she was tightening her lips and encouraging wrinkles, and deliberately relaxed her mouth, easing her irritation with thoughts of Neil, who had more than made up for his stubborn sister. In a few more years he would be in the mill's counting house, learning to take over from Fergus.

It was almost time to start looking for a suitable wife for him. He would make a good marriage, and it would no doubt be easy enough to find a wealthy husband for the girl — a strong-minded man who didn't object to a wife with a mind of her own. At least Rowena had good looks, so it shouldn't be too difficult to marry her off well, Sarah reflected, and waved graciously to an acquaintance, her mind moving to thoughts of wedding dresses.

*

At dinner that night Neil merely pushed the food about his plate, glancing from time to time at the sideboard clock, an elaborate timepiece mounted on the back of a black ebony elephant and topped by a colourful Chinaman with a parasol. Sarah, piqued because her dress-maker had not yet received the material for her new dress from London, said little. Fergus rarely spoke at the table.

For her part, Rowena thought nostalgically of the meals she had eaten in the nursery, listening to the town gossip that Ibby soaked up like a sponge, then relayed to her.

When the meal was over Fergus retired to his library as usual and Neil went out hurriedly.

In the drawing room Sarah flicked restlessly through the

pages of a novel, while Rowena worked on a sampler that Sarah had given her for her birthday. Fergus, to her surprise, had presented her with a pretty little cameo brooch. Neil and her father had forgotten the occasion.

Sarah went to bed early, with a headache, and Rowena was at last free to go to the peace and privacy of her own room and her books.

She envied Neil his opportunity to go to the Grammar School. She herself had attended a dame school until she was twelve, and now paid visits each morning to a governess, an impoverished lady of good breeding, to learn music, French, and sewing.

Her thirst for knowledge had to be patchily appeased by reading. Neil was willing enough to let her use his school-books, and she had helped him with his work on many occasions. Fergus, when he realised how much she enjoyed reading, had given her permission to use his library.

Sarah had chosen for her a selection of classical books, together with a smattering of the light romantic novels she herself preferred. She had loaned her several volumes of poetry, including the bound poems of Robert Tannahill, most famous of the Paisley poets. Tannahill, a weaver, had drowned a few months before the canal boat disaster. It was said that he had killed himself because of a thwarted love affair; this was one of the reasons why Sarah was so attached to his work, though she had never troubled to make his acquaintance or read his poetry while he was alive.

They would all have been shocked to know that for the moment Rowena had shunned the wide selection of reading material available to her and was avidly studying the writings of Thomas Payne, a strong believer in the ordinary working man's right to control his own destiny instead of being at the beck and call of his so-called superiors.

Absorbed now in Payne's fiery words she read on while the hours flowed by. It was quite late when she heard the front door opening, then the sound of a voice raised in song. She put the book down and went to the top of the staircase.

Below, the candles set in branched brackets around the hall flickered in the draught from the gaping front door. Neil swayed slightly in the middle of the square hall, waving a pamphlet over his head. As she hurried down the stairs he looked up and broke off his song.

'We've done for him! We've taught him a lesson!'

'What in God's name—?' said Fergus from the library door just as Mistress Cochrane bustled across the hall from the kitchen quarters to shut the open door.

Neil brandished the paper again. 'Old Bonaparte! The news has just come in — he attacked our army at Waterloo and they gave him a skelp on the lug that'll make his head ring for the rest of his days!'

To Rowena's horror he burst into a bawdy ditty about Napoleon Bonaparte, one that she had heard before in the streets. The housekeeper's face was a mask of outrage.

'Mistress Cochrane — away to your bed,' Fergus ordered, and the woman turned and almost ran. 'You're drunk, boy!'

'And what red-blooded man wouldn't drink to old Wellington tonight, tell me that, sir?'

'Neil — come to your bed—' Afraid to look at Fergus, Rowena went to her brother. He smelled of ale and tobacco and the thick stale air of the drinking dens.

'I'm not a child!' he said pettishly, pulling himself free of her restraining hand and weaving his way towards the stairs. Then he stumbled and only just saved himself from falling headlong. This time he didn't object when she pulled his arm about her shoulders and helped him up to his room, aware that Fergus, still standing at the library door, was watching them every degrading step of the way.

For a wonder Sarah hadn't heard the noise. Neil fell onto his bed as soon as she managed to get his jacket off. He was asleep by the time he was freed from his boots.

She drew the quilt over him, blew the lamp out, and left him to his drunken sleep, the pamphlet announcing Wellington's great victory at Waterloo still clutched firmly in one hand.

Fergus's voice grunted in reply to her tap on the library door. He was sitting by the fire, a glass of whisky and a book on the small table by his hand.

'I apologise for my brother's behaviour.'

He looked at her from beneath heavy brows then said, most

unexpectedly, 'I always thought he took after your mother, with his black hair and his fine skin, but you've got her eyes — and her nature. Are you happy here?'

'You've been very good to us, sir.'

'Can you not find some other title?' His voice was sharp with a gruff irritation.

'There is no other title,' she said helplessly.

'I suppose not. Good night to you.' He rose and went to the door, holding it open with a courtesy that both touched and pleased her.

'Neil's got a lot to learn, but don't be too vexed with the lad,' he said as she was going past him. 'The Duke's victory's gone to his head. He'll not be the only one who's going to find the morning light hard to take.'

'Kerr Fraser's brother's with Wellington's troops,' she suddenly recalled. They looked at each other for a long moment before Fergus said heavily, 'Then you'd best pray for him tonight.'

She did, before she turned out the lamp and got into bed. An owl hooted in the garden. She turned restlessly, and saw the silky gleam from the new stockings, hanging over the back of a chair.

At last she fell asleep, her last thought with Philip Fraser, and Alison.

VII

Watson and Bain's cotton mill was a tall grey-stone building five storeys high, standing on the site of an old bleachfield to the south-east of the town centre.

The lade taking water away from the river for the bleachfield's use had been deepened and strengthened to form a mill race that turned an overshot wheel some twenty feet in diameter. Not far from the manufactory itself stood a building that had once been the handsome residence of the bleachfield's owner, but was now used as the counting house.

Wide-eyed, determined to see all she could now that she had finally won permission to accompany Neil on his tour of the mill, Rowena followed her brother and Fergus Bain over the wooden bridge that gave employees access to the building, which was on the opposite side of the river to the old town.

The rattle and thump of machinery was all about them as soon as they went in through the big doors.

'The water-wheel,' Fergus explained, and opened another door to disclose a chamber filled with a complex series of revolving drums and cogs. Here, the noise was louder and underlined by the swish of water as the great wheel on the other side of the wall turned in the mill lade.

'I'll not explain the workings of it—' Amusement came swiftly to his dark eyes and he added, just as Rowena opened her mouth to protest, '—though I'm sure you'd grasp it easily enough. Suffice to say that through these cogs and belts and shafts water-power can reach any part of the mill.'

He opened a door, revealing a big store-room, its walls hidden by great bales. Some men and boys working in the room glanced up then went back to their work.

'This is where the cotton is brought into the mill. You see the hoist there, where the bales are taken up to the scutching room above.' He indicated the wooden platform and the pulleys vanishing through a large square hole in the ceiling above. 'The hoist goes right to the top of the building through a series of stores, one above another, each holding the cotton in different stages of manufacture. Now we'll go to the next floor.'

The wooden stairs were old and worn into smooth hollows by hundreds of thousands of feet climbing them over the years. As Rowena followed Fergus up into the warm gloom, clutching the banister tightly, she felt as though she was advancing into the pulsing throbbing heart of a living entity — an entity, she suddenly thought, that daily swallowed up some five hundred human beings of all ages and spat them out twelve hours later after sucking the energy from their very bones.

'The scutching room's situated over the store—' Fergus nodded at a closed door before turning away from it. 'No need for you to go in there. The carding machines are—'

But Rowena was determined to see everything. She marched to the door of the scutching room and opened it.

It was like walking into a snowstorm. She glimpsed, through a moving grey fog, a great revolving drum that almost filled the room. Shafts and wheels and belts connected it to the water machinery directly below, rattling the worn flooring. The drum was attended by men and boys, feeding it with cotton.

From the other end the cotton emerged in a continual thick grey fluffy blanket. Fibres covered the floor, clung to the workmen's clothes, filled the air in a cloud that almost immediately clogged Rowena's nose and mouth, setting up a fit of uncontrollable coughing.

She was seized from behind by the scruff of the neck, as though she was a wayward urchin rather than a young woman of fifteen, and bundled back onto the landing. The door of the scutching room was firmly closed; while Neil banged her on the back, Fergus brushed fluff off her skirt and from her hair.

'Now you know why I advised against going in there,' he said blandly as he worked.

The coughing subsided; she drew in a deep, shaky breath and removed a lump of fluff that clung to her lashes, obscuring her vision.

'How can they bear to work in that atmosphere?'

'They need to eat, and food costs money.' His voice was dry. 'They get used to it quickly. The scutching machine breaks the cotton bales down and clears out the trash. In the old days women had to do the work with sticks, so as you'll see, we've progressed.' He gave her skirt one last flick of the fingers, then turned to the other side of the landing.

'Here we have the carding machines, where the cotton begins to be transformed into a yarn.'

'You look like a half-plucked chicken,' Neil said disapprovingly to his sister as they followed Fergus into a vast room filled with water-operated machinery worked by women and children.

Here, too, there was a dusty haze in the air, motes drifting in the light from the long windows.

'A ventilation system draws most of the dust through pipes and out of the building, while fresh air is drawn in on all floors,' Fergus, who was watching Rowena's face, again intervened just as she began to speak. She closed her lips, and saw sudden amusement in his eyes.

The third floor held more carding machines and the drawing, roving and stretching machinery. Rowena had never realised how many stages cotton had to go through before it reached the spinning jeanies, a thousand of them housed on the fourth and fifth floors, each one hand operated, with a hundred spindles.

Men and women tended the machines, whose whirling spindles were controlled by large wheels at the side of each spinning jeanie. Children, some of them quite small, dragged baskets of cotton bobbins to and from the machines, or worked at piecing broken threads together, or crouched beneath the jeanies themselves, cleaning them and gathering up waste.

Neil's nose wrinkled fastidiously at the rancid tang in the room.

'We keep the oil to a minimum, and burn tar twice a week to counteract the smell,' Fergus shouted above the noise of the jeanies. The whole building shook with noise, Rowena thought; the thump and splash of the water-wheel, the crash and clack of machinery. The very walls seemed to vibrate. It was little wonder that the workers all had withdrawn, absorbed faces,

and had scarcely bothered to glance at the visitors. She
shuddered at the prospect of having to spend long hours in such
a hot, noisy, rancid atmosphere.

A small group had gathered round one machine that had
come to a standstill. Fergus began to strip off his jacket.

'Wait for me outside—' she saw, rather than heard, him say
above the noise, before he crouched down to examine the
machinery. Neil turned at once and made for the door, but she
lingered, walking the length of the huge room to the windows at
the end.

From the fifth floor the grimy panes gave a view of the aque-
duct carrying the canal across the river. There was a gig-boat
going over as she stood looking out. She watched it disappear
behind the bushes that lined the canal. Someone touched her
arm and she turned to see Fergus, jacket in hand. Neil was waiting for them on the landing outside, his nose wrinkled with
distaste.

'The noise and the smell's enough to turn a man's stomach,'
he complained.

'You'll get used to it,' Fergus told him, adding wryly, as Neil
started down the steep wooden stairway before them, 'Think of
it as the smell of money, lad, and your stomach'll soon grow to
appreciate it.'

Neil went on without answering. He had reached the bottom
floor and Rowena, followed by Fergus, had only a few steps to
go, when the store-room door opened and a man, his arms filled
with spindles, came out.

He put one foot on the bottom step, realised that there were
people coming down, and stepped aside.

'Father—' Rowena hurried down the last four treads and
arrived beside him, catching Neil's arm, and drawing him with
her as she went.

'Father, it's me, Rowena. And here's Neil—'

Fergus stopped on the stairs above them, remote from the
family group, but watching closely as, for the first time in years,
Ewan Lindsay and his son came face to face.

Ewan, once the tallest man in the world in Rowena's eyes,
now stooped by premature ageing, had to look up at the handsome, well-dressed youth before him.

The shadow of a smile passed over the older man's face. His lips fluttered, parted.

Neil didn't look at his father. 'For God's sake, Rowena,' he said, his voice crisp with anger. Two spots of colour flared in his pale face. His eyes were shards of ice as he dragged his arm from hers and turned away.

It was though a curtain had been dropped over Ewan's face. He dipped his head in a vague gesture that might have been acknowledgement, might have been deference. Then he pushed past Rowena and up the stairs with a muttered excuse.

'How could you?' Forgetting Fergus's presence, forgetting everything but the way Ewan had seemed to shrink beneath Neil's contemptuous look, she rounded on her brother. 'He's our father!'

He looked as though he would like to shake her. 'No! He belongs to a life we left behind years ago. Can you never accept that it's over—?'

'The counting house next — you'll be impatient to see where you're going to work, Neil — 'Fergus said blandly, opening the mill door to let them pass. Rowena saw that his eyes, resting on the back of Neil's head, were coolly disapproving.

VIII

The house standing on the mill site had once been an elegant home, but now it was shabby through neglect, its graceful, high-ceilinged rooms used to house the counting house and the schoolroom.

The counting house was at the front, its air clearer than that of the mill, but no less stuffy, for the tall dirty windows were tightly shut. Instead of the rumble and thump of machinery this place was filled with the dry sound of quills scratching and rustling as they hurried over paper.

At the rear of the house, reached by a dark passage, a large room, formerly the servants' pantry, was used for the schooling of the mill workers' children.

A brave attempt had been made to brighten it. The floor was swept, the big clumsy fireplace, empty in the summer months, had been black-leaded until it shone, and there were a few pictures pinned to the walls. Books and slates and pencils were neatly stacked on a shelf.

'Most of the younger employees work till seven in the evening then attend here for an hour before going home—' Fergus explained as he led the way into the room. 'During the day Mistress Brodie here teaches the smallest children so that their mothers can be free to work. And she supervises them in the few tasks they can already carry out.'

A group of infants, some little more than babies, it seemed to Rowena, were squatting on the wooden floor, busily employed, heads bent over their work. The girl who sat on a chair in the middle of the group, reading aloud from a well-thumbed book, stood up hastily as her visitors came in, greeting them with a shy smile.

Etta Brodie lived with her parents in Burn Row, near Gordon's Loan, and Rowena knew her by sight. She was small and slight and still very young. Her high-waisted brown dress was serviceable, clean, and neatly darned here and there.

Her small oval face seemed to float in a sea of thick black hair. Her long-lashed eyes were large and bright and green. Her slightly hollowed cheeks had a flush that looked healthy, but spoke of the consumptive condition that was all too common in Paisley.

'Mistress Brodie worked in one of the spinning rooms,' Fergus explained. 'But the fluff proved to be bad for her chest and so she was moved here, where the air is better.'

'What are the children doing?' Perplexed, Rowena studied the leather strips, the protective rags bound about the children's small fingers, the hundreds of pieces of sharp metal piled in the centre of the small group, by the teacher's chair.

'Setting metal teeth into leather for the carding machines.' The girl's low voice had an attractive huskiness to it.

'But surely that's too dangerous a task for such tiny hands—'

Impatience cracked like a whip in Fergus's voice, causing

swift, anxious colour to flame in the schoolmistress's thin face and the children, gazing curiously at the newcomers, to duck their heads over their work again. 'Only small fingers can do it properly, and it's quite safe, once they learn how to go about it. Am I not right, Mistress Brodie?'

'Quite safe, sir,' the girl hurried to agree.

'We pay them, of course,' Fergus added. 'And they learn their lessons as they work.'

Annoyed with herself for having alarmed the girl and her charges, Rowena smiled at Etta, and indicated the book in her hand. 'What are you reading to them?'

The school-mistress held the book out to her, but before Rowena could take it Neil's hand reached for the little volume. Startled, Etta Brodie surrendered it to him.

'I remember this—' he flipped through the pages swiftly. 'Look, Rowena – you used to read these stories to me when I was ill. We still have the book somewhere.'

'This copy is very old—' Etta said breathlessly, apologetically, taking the book back and smoothing the worn, greasy cover with nervous fingers. 'But the children love it, so I allow them one story each day, while they're working.'

'If you wish, you can have my copy,' Neil offered.

'Oh—!' In her sudden, surprised pleasure the girl tilted her head on its slender neck and looked up at him fully for the first time, her green eyes sparkling, her lips curving into a shy smile. 'I would – the children would so appreciate—' Her stammered gratitude was interrupted by an attack of coughing that forced her to bow her head again and lift a corner of her checkered shawl to her lips.

'Then I shall bring the book tomorrow,' said Neil, with a gentleness to his voice that Rowena had never heard before.

As Fergus led them out of the room to see the water-wheel that powered the carding and roving and scutching machinery Neil turned back to smile once more at the girl.

Outside, they crossed the cobbled yard, with its tufts of grass tenaciously growing in every crack, to where the mill lade was diverted from the river to feed and turn the great wheel.

Standing on the small wooden inspection platform built over the lade Rowena watched, fascinated, as the iron buckets set all round the rim filled with water flowing from above them. As each bucket filled it dropped and the next took its place; and so the continual spill of water, seemingly so light beside the wood and iron mechanism, kept the wheel turning ceaselessly, tirelessly.

'How do you stop it?' she wanted to know, and Fergus, pleased by her interest, explained that the water-flow could be stopped by closing the sluice-gates at the junction of the river and the lade.

Neil frowned thoughtfully at the wheel. 'Isn't there enough water here to power the entire mill? Why aren't the spinning-jeanies worked by water as well? That way you'd need fewer employees.'

Fergus glanced at him with faint surprise.

'Yes, we could easily power all the jeanies. But that means that the entire mill could be brought to a standstill if there's no water to turn the wheel in a summer drought, or if the river freezes in winter. As long as the spinning jeanies can be worked by hand they need never stop. If necessary we can buy roving from the steam-powered carding machines in Lancashire for the jeanies to spin.'

Then, with a glance at Rowena, he added, 'And I doubt if your sister would approve of your eagerness to lay off workers.'

Neil, looking up at the building looming above them, was too busy with his own thoughts to pay any heed. 'It would make even more sense to install steam power.'

Rowena saw Fergus's lids droop as though to hide his expression, but his voice was patient when he said, 'That would cost more capital than we have in hand.'

'But it would pay dividends.' There was an avaricious gleam in Neil's blue eyes. 'Isn't that what business is all about — making profits?'

'It would pay dividends eventually, but this mill does well enough. Paisley's a settled town, and it should be left as it is. A few short years ago the spinning here was done by women in their own homes. Now see how much more is done with the machinery we have. And the looms are still worked by men in small weaving shops attached to their houses. You can't say the shawl industry's been harmed by that, can you? Best not to hurry progress. It'll come soon enough.'

'Too soon for some,' Rowena said bleakly.

'And not fast enough for others,' Neil told her, and went to look at the sluice gates. Seeing that some cotton still clung to her fine red Paisley shawl, Rowena took it off and shook it. The dislodged fluff floated free, some of it drifting down to where the water thundered from sluice to wheel. The cotton that brushed the surface was immediately whipped out of sight.

Fergus took the shawl from her, gave it a final vigorous shake, and tucked it carefully about her shoulders.

'I admire your brother's head for business, but it takes more than that to run a mill like this. He needs to care about the machinery as well.'

She gazed after Neil's tall, straight-backed figure, uneasiness welling up in her. It seemed to her that Neil's interest lay more in spending money, or gambling it away, than in earning it.

'I'm beginning to think,' Fergus was saying thoughtfully, 'that if his interest only lies with the counting house it might be as well to bring young Fraser back into the mill itself. The manager I've got's getting old, like myself, and beginning to find it all too much.'

'Kerr Fraser?' Her heart gave an excited skip.

'He's good with machinery and he's been on the road long enough—' Fergus said thoughtfully, staring down into the foaming water.

'Come on!' Neil shouted from the bridge, and Fergus broke out of his reverie and led the way from the platform.

'I trust you've enjoyed your visit to the mill, since you were so eager to see it,' he said as they crossed the yard.

'How can folk work in such surroundings, day after day, year after year?'

There was an edge to his voice. 'We keep the place as clean and well-ventilated as we can. We don't employ pauper children as many other mill-owners do. We provide our employees' children with schooling—'

'So that their mothers can come and work for you in the mill. And so that the children, in their turn, will work for you.'

'The women need to earn money if they're to feed their families.'

'Pay men more, and let them support their wives and children themselves.'

He gave a short laugh, half angry, half amused. 'You'd stand the country's economy and well-being on its head, just for the sake of a Utopian dream? It's not given to you, or to me, lassie, to change the ways of the world. And I must admit that, for myself, I've no quarrel with them as they are.'

It was noon. A whistle shrilled from inside the mill as Fergus left them and went back to the counting house. Workers came streaming out of the building to cross the bridge. Most of them lived nearby, and were able to snatch a few minutes at home before going back to their machines.

A small group of children stood together in the street; a girl much the same age as Rowena had been when she lost her mother, two smaller children by her side, a tiny infant wrapped in a shawl clutched in her arms.

The girl looked with brief curiosity at the well-dressed young people walking across the bridge, then her eyes brightened as she saw the face she sought, somewhere behind them.

As she and Neil began the walk to Carriagehill Rowena looked back and saw a young woman detach herself from the crowd flooding over the bridge. She went to the children, took the baby from its sister, and hurried, followed by her little family, into a quiet corner, her back to the street. There was just time, Rowena realised, for her to put her baby to the breast before going back to work.

IX

Although she was a regular visitor to his mother's home, Rowena's first meeting with Kerr after his return to Paisley took place at a dinner party in the Bains' house, held to mark a double event — Neil's entry to the mill counting-house, and Kerr's new duties as mill manager.

He was the last guest to arrive; the others, ex-Provost Orr, the first man to hold the Provost's office in Paisley, Mistress Orr, Mister Andrew MacKenzie, shawl manufacturer, his wife and pretty daughter, and Maxwell King, a banker who had formerly been Fergus's partner, had all bowled up to the door in their carriages and been greeted by Sarah and Fergus.

Their hostess then swept them into the drawing-room with a murmured instruction to Rowena to wait for their final guest.

She paced the hall, well aware of the way her stomach fluttered and her breath caught in her throat at each imagined sound of wheels on gravel. She longed for, and yet dreaded, this first meeting for years. Part of her was still the angry little girl who had stormed 'I hate you!' at him, the day he told her that she was not going to persuade his mother to take her in. And the other part of her belonged to today — a girl blossoming into womanhood, keenly aware that from the moment he had plucked her from the water in the canal basin and given her life back to her, Kerr Fraser had become involved in that life, whether he liked it or not.

And whether she herself liked it or not, come to that, she thought, then jumped as the door knocker rattled.

Without thinking, she went to answer the summons, opening the door just as Ibby came scurrying from the back of the hall.

'Mistress Rowena—!' the little maid hissed as she sped over the carpet. 'I'm supposed to do that!'

'Oh—!' Suddenly mindful that her place was that of hostess,

not servant, Rowena began to close the door again, scarcely noticing, in her confusion, the tall figure that had already taken a step forward.

Something offered resistance to the closing door and there was a muffled exclamation from the other side of the panels. Ibby tried to edge her respectfully aside and open the door, and for a ludicrous moment the two of them battled against each other before Ibby, throwing respect to the winds, nudged her young mistress out of the way with a bony elbow and swept the door wide.

'Come in, sir.'

Kerr Fraser, taller than Rowena remembered, far better looking than Rowena remembered, and infinitely more mature and self-assured than Rowena remembered, paused for a moment on the step, looking from one girl to the other, his mobile mouth curving upwards into a quickly-subdued grin, his eyebrows arching.

'Are you quite certain? Or is this a trap you've set so that you can crush my toes a second time?'

'Kerr — please come in. I — you took me by surprise. I had been listening for your carriage wheels coming up the drive—' She told herself furiously that she was babbling, and clasped her hands before her to still their fluttering, enraged with the juvenile stupidity that had allowed her to make such a nonsense of their first proper meeting.

'I walked up from the town. I don't as yet aspire to a carriage. Nor am I old and infirm enough, as yet, to require one.' He advanced into the hall, tall and erect and confident, removing his tall hat as he came.

Ibby closed the door with a decisive thump and followed along behind him to take his hat, her nose positively glowing with her own embarrassment over the confusion, her eyes snapping accusingly at Rowena as she flounced off and left the two of them alone.

'Rowena?' Kerr held out both his hands and she had no option but to unclasp her fingers and let him take them in his own strong warm grip. He studied her with open interest; she resisted the temptation to lower her eyes demurely before his gaze, and instead lifted her chin and returned look for look, scrutiny for scrutiny, glad that she had decided to wear her new gown, a blue silk dress with the Paisley shawl pine pattern richly woven in reds, deep golds, and shades of green on the bodice and short sleeves, and round the bottom of the skirt.

She liked what she saw. The years away from home had turned him from a gawky, serious boy to a well-travelled, assured man. His hair was russet brown now, but the June sun had teased gold streaks through its thick wavy mass. His eyes were as clear and direct as ever, his face ruggedly handsome, and his mouth had a pleasing uplift at the corners, as though he smiled often.

He wore blue trousers and a dark green coat, cut so that it revealed his ruffled shirt and embroidered blue waistcoat. A foam of spotless white lace at his throat seemed to accentuate, rather than soften, the firm lines of his face, and the candles in their branched holders picked out the gold lights in his hair as he nodded approvingly.

'My mother said that you'd grown to be a pretty young woman. She's wrong—' His eyes moved again over her face, lingering on each feature, and she felt a pleasant thrill run through her at the open admiration she read in his gaze. '—You've become quite beautiful.'

His Scots accent was as strong as ever, she noted with approval. The shawl industry had resulted in considerable trade between Paisley and England; a number of people from South of the border had made their homes in the weaving town in the past ten years or so, and more than a few of the townspeople travelled regularly to London and the great Northern textile mills.

Altogether too many of them, in Rowena's opinion, returned from the South affecting an English drawl that sat uncomfortably on their tongues. But not Kerr Fraser.

'But I've no doubt that you've already been told that by numerous admirers,' he was saying now.

She felt her brows twitch together with irritation, and would have withdrawn her hands from his if his grasp hadn't been so firm. 'There's more to life than courting.'

She hadn't forgotten the way his face lit up when he was amused. 'Indeed? You're surely not going to devote yourself to good works, are you? Has religion got you by the throat already? I warn you, Rowena,' he teased, 'it can spoil a woman's beauty.'

'So I gathered from my step-mother,' she said dryly, and his smile broadened abruptly, disintegrated, and split into a peal of surprised and delighted laughter.

'So – you've a quick tongue as well as beauty?' he asked when he had recovered. 'That makes it even harder to believe that you've managed to keep the suitors at bay.'

'Perhaps we both shy from the thought of marriage. I notice you've not brought a wife home with you, after all those years away.'

His mouth twitched again, but his voice was suitably solemn when he said 'The choice was considerable, and the English lassies sweet and biddable enough, but even so—' His eyes drifted over her face again with a look that set her heart and mind into a whirl of sweet confusion. But something contrary in her nature, or perhaps some sense of insecurity, took hold of her.

'Even so—' she picked up the words he had set drifting in the air between them '—you stayed true to your Paisley love.'

'My—?' His brows lifted in silent interrogation.

'Eliza Wilson. Wasn't that her name?'

All at once his face was closed to her. He released her hands.

'I mind the girl. She left Paisley soon after I did, I believe,' he said shortly. 'I've no notion where she may be now.'

The drawing-room doors opened, letting out a gust of voices and laughter, and Sarah came into the hall, her blue eyes sweeping over Kerr as she advanced, her mouth curving into the coquettish smile she reserved for attractive men.

'Kerr Fraser!'

'Mistress Bain—' He swept a courtly bow, took her hand in his and kissed it with a natural, unself-conscious grace that brought a flush of pleasure to Sarah's cheeks. Then he straightened and told her 'You've not changed in all the time I've been away.'

'But you have,' said Sarah, archly demure. 'You've gained a most pleasing maturity – and you've learned the art of flattery while you were in England.'

'I assure you, Mistress Bain, that I've merely learned to appreciate a beautiful woman when I see one.'

He offered her his arm and the two of them swept into the drawing-room, leaving Rowena, cursing her wayward tongue for running away with itself and mentioning Eliza Wilson, to trail after them.

*

In the dining-room candle-light sparkled on silver, struck off voluptuously-rounded china and fluted glasses, and picked out brilliant bursts of colour from Sarah's jewelled finger rings with each gesture of her white hands.

She was a talented hostess, making herself the centre-piece round which all the others pivoted, but even so Rowena was aware of Maxwell King's gaze fixed on her from across the snowy tablecloth.

Maxwell, a lean, dark Englishman, had first made his home in Paisley as works manager at Watson and Bain's manufactory, then run a small mill of his own at Barrhead, several miles further up the River Cart, before turning to banking. A widower in his early forties, he had been paying special attention to Rowena each time they met for the past six months.

Sarah was talking about the house she had recently persuaded Fergus to buy in Helensburgh, a seaside town some forty miles from Paisley.

The soft light flattered her, and gave her a youthful bloom. Although she had put on weight over the past three years she still favoured light muslin dresses with low necklines that emphasised her creamy bosom.

'Murdo says the air in Helensburgh's quite the best—'

'Aye, there's a school of thought that claims sea air is beneficial,' Murdo Latimer, the Bains' physician, set down his glass of claret. 'Fergus, you must let Sarah persuade you to visit Helensburgh. It may well ease those aches and pains of yours.'

His wife chimed in, smiling at Maxwell, well pleased with the opportunity to air the medical knowledge she had gained second-hand. 'Paisley has a damp climate, you see, not conducive to good health.'

'A pity, since that very dampness is so well suited to textile manufacture.' Maxwell commented. 'Murdo's right, Fergus – you've surely earned the right to think of yourself instead of the manufactory, now that you've got Neil and Kerr to see to things for you.'

'I wish I could do the same,' Andrew MacKenzie said sourly, 'Paisley's not a healthy place to be now there's revolution in the air.'

Sarah shivered, genuine fear touching her pale blue eyes. 'You don't think we could go the same way as the French?'

'There's a very great difference between France and Paisley,' her husband growled.

Neil had scarcely spoken until now. 'The British working class has more sense than to try revolution.'

'An empty belly and fear for his family can change a man's viewpoint,' Kerr said, and Neil's mouth took on a derisive twist.

'You've been out of the town for the past eight years, Fraser. You're hardly an authority on the Paisley folk now.'

Rowena saw Kerr's fine grey eyes flash irritation at her brother before being carefully hooded. 'I've spent those years travelling the length and breadth of the country. Unrest's in the air — in Paisley as well as elsewhere.'

'Tumbrils rattling along the High Street?' Neil jeered. 'A guillotine at the market cross—?'

'Never!' Murdo's practical wife said at once, and the physician nodded.

'The British aren't hot-blooded young men, nor are they dimwits. The working folk may grumble now and again but they'd not turn against their King and country as the French did.'

'Nor would they be able,' Neil added. 'They know the militia would be down on them before they'd time to raise a single standard.'

'You think you can keep the majority of your countrymen down by force for ever?' Kerr asked, with a veiled contempt that brought a flush to Neil's handsome face.

The words were on Rowena's lips before she could stop them. 'How can you expect them to hold their tongues while wages are cut and the Government pushes up the price of the bread they badly need to feed their bairns?'

Eleven pairs of eyes turned to her. She looked down at her

plate, feeling like an animal that had been chased into a corner and trapped.

'I think you'd be wise to leave such matters to those who know more about them, lassie—' Ex-Provost Orr spoke with measured deliberation.

'But it's true that wages have gone down, is it not? And the Corn Law's forced up the price of bread. The two make uneasy partners. When folk get hungry—'

'My argument exactly — and put very well.' Kerr said, and she flushed as he favoured her with an unexpectedly warm smile.

'That's scarcely our fault,' Andrew MacKenzie protested. 'You must recall that a great number of Paisley men came home from the Army all at the one time. That made for a glut of skilled workers in the town.'

His choice of argument was unfortunate. 'So you think another war's the answer? Indeed, sir, it would be one way to kill off the unwanted men.' Kerr's voice was suddenly taut. 'The trouble is that sometimes it only maims them, and then they become a burden on us, do they not?'

There was an awkward silence as they all recollected his younger brother Philip, home these four years after the fighting at Waterloo, his scarred face bitter and much older than his years, a maimed hand making it impossible for him to return to his loom.

MacKenzie had the grace to look embarrassed as his wife glared at him.

'Rowena's right,' Kerr spoke into the silence. 'You can't keep hungry folk down. If they choose to follow the French example—'

'We'll teach them a lesson. That's all there is to it.' Neil held his empty glass out for more wine.

'It might not be as easy as all that!' Kerr sounded as though he was on the verge of losing his temper. 'They're human beings, with as much right to food and shelter and the essentials of life as you and me!'

'You're over-keen to voice their arguments.' There was a clear warning in Maxwell's voice. 'Remember that you're one of the masters in Watson and Bain's mill now. It would be foolish of you to take the side of the rabble if it should ever come to a disturbance.'

'Remember which side my bread's buttered on? Aye, I'll do that – but it doesn't stop me from thinking there's a lot of sense spoken by those who claim that if folk aren't given their rights they'll be driven to take them, as they were in France.'

'We'll not see revolution in Paisley,' Fergus stepped in. 'The new ways haven't come north of the Border yet. There are very few steam engines here, for one thing. Our folk have no reason to resort to smashing machinery like the Luddites in England. The employers here are fair men.'

Then he planted his hands on the table and clumsily pushed himself to his feet before lifting his glass.

'And now, I ask you to drink to the continuing prosperity of Watson and Bain, and to the success of the two young men who've invested their futures in the mill. Neil and Kerr – may they prosper, despite these troubled times.'

Over the rim of her glass Rowena watched the two young men as she drank the toast. Her brother was flushed with wine and heady with Moira MacKenzie's admiration; Kerr Fraser kept his eyes fixed on the table as the guests drank his health.

As the party moved back to the drawing-room Sarah graciously accepted a flurry of compliments on her hospitality.

'Was it not Rowena who planned this evening for you, Sarah?' her husband asked innocently.

Her eyes were angry, but her voice sweet. 'I was just about to tell them so.'

'Then we must thank Rowena for an excellent dinner—' Maxwell claimed her hand with practised skill and brushed his lips lightly over her fingers before turning to Sarah and taking her bejewelled fingers '—and you, my dear Sarah, for teaching your ward to be as superb a hostess as yourself.'

Mollified, Sarah beamed as her hand, in its turn, was kissed.

'Aye, Maxwell – you've not lost the English way with words, for all that you've spent so many years among the thick-tongued Scots,' Fergus said dryly.

The kiss, the first salutation of its kind that she had received, tingled against Rowena's fingers. Surreptitiously, embarrassed by the older man's attentions, she brushed the memory of it off against the cool silk of her skirt, then looked up to see Kerr's amused eyes on her. He looked deliberately down at her hand, now innocently smoothing her gown, then back at her face, one eyebrow quirked.

'Can you really be so inexperienced that a man's flattery throws you into turmoil?' that eyebrow seemed to say. Angry, on the defensive, she made a move towards him, then out of the corner of her eye she saw Fergus, who had just begun to make his way slowly out of the dining room, stagger and catch at the back of a chair.

Swiftly she went to give him support, but Kerr, too, had seen what was happening, and he was there before her, offering his arm. She saw Fergus nod gratefully, and knew that he was leaning most of his weight on the younger man as the two of them moved slowly across the hall in front of her.

In the drawing room the company clustered about Sarah at first, then gradually separated into groups, each little knot untying itself and scattering to form other knots as the evening wore on. Kerr, recently arrived as he was from travelling among the textile centres in England, was claimed in conversation by his employer and the shawl-manufacturer, then by Sarah.

Maxwell King came to sit by Rowena and turned out to be an easy man to talk to, once she managed to forget that he was a friend and contemporary of Fergus's, and overcome her feeling of awe.

A widower for many years, and a man without children, he lived in a fine house not far from the one they sat in now. He, too, had travelled far, spending time in France and the Netherlands in his youth. He had a gift for painting pictures with words that enthralled Rowena.

When Sarah imperiously summoned him to her side and Rowena was alone again she felt a strange sensation, as though she had been on some great journey to lands where the people spoke English with strange accents, and had then been returned, abruptly, to the drawing-room.

'Now I can understand why Mister Bain's decided to leave the running of the counting-house and the mill to Neil and myself,' Kerr sat down beside her, his eyes on his host, who was comfortably settled in his favourite chair by the fire. 'He seems to have aged more years than I've been away.'

'The rheumatics have afflicted him badly those past two

years. Some days are worse than others, and the rainy weather we had all through May hasn't helped.'

'Poor man, it must be hard to have to rely on others after an active life.' Then he said wryly, 'I called in on your father when I got home. D'you still visit with him?'

'Every week, difficult though it is.'

'Aye, it is that. It fair made my flesh creep. I'd the feeling all the time I was in that house of his that there was a prayer staring out at me from beneath a chair, or a clutch of Catechisms ready to pounce from a corner like a pack of unfriendly dogs. And it's near impossible to hold a sensible conversation with that stepmother of yours around all the time.'

'Unless you're God,' Rowena suggested primly, and surprised him into another peal of laughter that caused heads to turn and eyebrows to lift.

'Does Neil ever go with you?' he asked, when he had sobered. She shook her head, and followed his gaze to where Neil talked with Moira MacKenzie, the shawl-manufacturer's daughter.

'They make a handsome couple. It'd be a good match — the shawl industry and the thread industry,' he said, and grinned down at her.

'Maybe.' She had no doubt that that was what the Bains had in mind. Moira and her parents were frequent visitors, and the girl obviously thought highly of Neil. But it was difficult to know what he himself wanted. He still disappeared for hours on end when he wasn't at the counting-house, but nowadays he seldom brought back the smoky, alcoholic smell of the ale-houses with him when he returned. There was a new air of happiness and excitement about him. Watching him now, smiling at something Moira had said, she thought of the empty spaces on her bookshelf where the books she and Neil had had as children had once stood, and wondered, not for the first time, if his new secrecy had anything to do with Etta Brodie, the shy, consumptive little school-mistress at the mill.

As though his train of thought followed closely on her own, Kerr said slowly 'I'm finding it hard to work with Neil. It seems to me that he lacks your — your understanding of folk. I doubt we're not going to find it easy, running the place between us.'

'You will, once you both settle to it.'

But a shadow had darkened Kerr's eyes, giving them the look of rain-heavy clouds. 'You think so? I get the feeling that he resents me coming back, interfering in all that he's set up for himself. It's as if he almost hates me.'

'That's nonsense!' But she had recently seen her brother's antagonism for herself, at the dinner table. Like Kerr, she was at a loss to understand it.

'You think so?' he asked now, then added, dourly, as Moira MacKenzie's laugh rippled across the room towards them, 'Maybe I'd get on better with the man if I was richer — and prettier — and a lassie into the bargain.'

X

There was an increasing air of unrest about Paisley as June gave way to July — a sense of revolution, no matter how much the employers and the Council might try to deny it.

A strange new feverish excitement stalked the town. It could be seen in the hot eyes of the young weavers as they gathered at the street corners, sensed in their very movements when they walked together, talking in low, intense voices.

The British working-class men wanted change. They wanted to be represented properly in Parliament, but the Government, terrified in case Britain should crumble into anarchy as France had, chose to ignore the situation in the hope that it would go away of its own accord.

'But it won't,' Philip Fraser said, pacing back and forth across his mother's kitchen floor with his strange lurching gait, tossing back the lank fair hair that fell over his forehead.

Rowena was a little afraid of Philip. His hooded eyes surveyed the world with a bitterness brought on by his Army experiences and by the wounds he had received at Waterloo, four years earlier. A jagged scar ran from beneath his hair to his jaw on the left side of his face, his left hand was missing the middle finger, and a permanently stiff leg gave him his unwieldy walk.

For Alison's and Kerr's sakes, Fergus Bain had taken Philip on in the mill store-room, a menial job that brought little into the house.

'They'll march — unless someone listens to what they have to say.' His voice rose, his eyes narrowed and took on the light that Rowena had seen in the eyes of the men at the street corners. 'And when they do, the authorities had better watch out—'

'Never!' His mother looked up from her knitting, real distress in her face. 'They've more sense in Paisley than to get caught up in revolution!'

'It's not a game, mother! It's men being pushed beyond endurance — men in Paisley as much as anywhere else!'

'For pity's sake, Philip—' Alison's protest ended in a sharp gasp. Her knitting wires fell to her lap, then to the floor as she pushed herself upright, clutching at the arm of her chair, fighting for breath.

Rowena flew to dip a cloth in cold water while Philip, his political fervour forgotten, supported his mother in his arms.

As Rowena sponged the older woman's pale, sweating face the gripping spasm slowed, then ceased. Alison drew a long ragged breath, straightened, and smiled weakly at the two frightened young faces.

'I'm fine. I just turned awkwardly and got a cramp.'

'You're not well,' Rowena fretted. 'You should see a physician.'

'Och, lassie, when you get to my age you must expect aches and twinges now and then!' Alison picked up her knitting then put it down again as she heard the shop door opening.

'I'll go,' Rowena said quickly, and left mother and son together. She often helped in the shop when she was visiting Gordon's Loan, and she had come to know the business well enough.

She weighed and wrapped sweets for two solemn-eyed children, took the penny, hot and sticky, from the older girl's hand, and watched them leave, her mind worrying all the time over Alison. She had been uneasy about the older woman for several weeks now.

When she went back to the kitchen Alison was up and about, bustling round the range. Kerr had come in; his eyebrows lifted as he saw Rowena step through the door leading from the shop.

'So — we have a new assistant? Business must be doing well, mother, for you to be able to afford the likes of Mistress Lindsay here.'

'Don't tease the lassie,' Alison ordered, her voice still a trifle shaky. She reached out to shift a pot from one side of the range to the other.'Rowena's helped me many a time when the shop was busy and I had nobody else to hand.'

'Here, I'll do that—' Rowena hurried to lift the pot. 'You should still be resting.'

'Why?' Kerr wanted to know at once, putting down the newspaper he had been looking at. 'Are you ill, mother?'

'It was just an attack of cramp,' Alison said lightly. 'Rowena fusses over me too much. But since you're so eager to help, lassie, you can bring me that crock of barley.'

Philip, his eyes hot with sudden jealousy, reached it first, lifting it down from the shelf, jostling past Rowena to take it to his mother. Then he turned and picked up her shawl from the back of a chair.

'You'd best be getting back to Carriagehill — before they send the servants out looking for you.'

There was a sneer in his voice that brought Kerr's head up from the newspaper he was reading. His grey eyes frosted, his lips parted, but before he could speak his mother's voice said sharply, 'Philip!'

The ex-soldier lifted one shoulder in a sulky shrug. 'I'm just telling the truth — Mistress Bain'll be wondering where she's got to.'

'I'll walk up the road with you, Rowena.' Kerr got up, took the cloak from his brother, and put it about her shoulders. Alison came to hug her, a silent apology in her eyes for her younger son's abrupt manner. Philip picked up the newspaper his brother had discarded, dropped into a chair by the kitchen table, and began to read.

'You must excuse Philip,' Kerr said when they were outside. 'The Army seems to have robbed him of what good manners he had.'

Easily, without fuss, he took her hand and drew it through the crook of his elbow. Her gloved fingers were pleasantly aware of the sinewy strength and maleness of the arm beneath the cloth of his coat sleeve.

'Mind you, I think there's a touch of jealousy there. My mother misses my sister sorely, and you've eased some of the pain. Somehow, Philip can't accept that.'

Since his return to the town he had often walked her home from the shop; sometimes, when they were both free of other commitments, they strolled along the river bank for a mile or two, Kerr talking about his travels, Rowena listening with rapt attention.

He had even allowed her to visit the mill on several occasions now that he was manager, taking time to give her a more detailed tour of the place than she had had with Fergus and Neil on her first day, explaining things with the enthusiasm of a man who loved his work and believed implicitily in its worth.

They had become friends, yet always there was something that came between them, making their eyes suddenly meet, then as suddenly break the look, or catching their shared laughter and stifling it in their throats, or giving her that self-conscious tingle if his fingers happened to brush against hers.

But now there was more on her mind than her confused feelings about Kerr, or the reasons for his brother's open dislike.

'Kerr, I'm concerned about your mother. She's not as well as she makes out.'

'Och, she's fine. It's just this moist air that bothers her now that she's getting older — nearly everyone in the town has a touch of the rheumatics, or a cough — or both.'

'It's more than that with her.'

'She's worn herself out with work, I know that.' He steered her past a group of gossiping housewives. 'I'll tell you something my mother doesn't know yet. I've taken a house in Barclay Street for her. It's more like the sort of house she deserves, and I can afford it now that I've been appointed manager in the mill.'

'What about the shop?'

'We'll close it,' he said firmly. 'She owns the property — we can sell it and maybe bring in enough to settle my father's debts once and for all. It's time she got the chance to live like a lady, the way she was meant to live.'

She looked up at him and saw that his jawline had hardened and there was new purpose in his clear eyes and the set of his mouth. He looked suddenly older.

'God knows she's worked hard enough these past years. I've been waiting a long time for the moment when I could take the load from her shoulders — and now the moment's come!'

A horse, a magnificent animal, clopped down the street towards them, its rider removing his beaver hat and bowing as he passed them. Rowena inclined her head in reply, recognising Maxwell King. His gaze flicked from her to the young man at her side, and he gave Kerr a nod of recognition before his eyes went back to Rowena. Then the hat was replaced on his smooth dark head, and he had passed them.

Kerr turned to watch him go. 'D'you see much of that banker?'

'He's a friend of Mister Bain — and Mistress Bain,' she added, remember the way Sarah fussed and flirted with Maxwell King each time he called. 'He and Mister Bain were in partnership at the mill once, I believe. Then Mister King ran his own mill near Barrhead before taking up banking.'

'D'you like him?'

'I've not given the matter much thought.'

'He seems to like you well enough,' Kerr said, a cool note creeping into his voice.

She was about to scoff at the idea, but just then she realised that they were about to pass by a group of young men, weavers from the district between Causewayside Street and Carriagehill. They stood in a tight knot at a street corner, eyeing Kerr and Rowena as they approached.

Looking into their truculent faces, seeing how closely they watched her as she walked towards them, Rowena suddenly became aware of the comparison between her fine clothes and their patched jackets and shabby shoes. She saw the gaunt, shadowed faces, some of them as young as her own, but marked by deprivation and worry, turned towards her, and instinctively she drew closer to her escort.

Kerr had already sensed her uneasiness. 'They'll not harm

you.' His hand tightened protectively, on her arm and he added reassuringly 'Not while I'm here to look after you.'

The fear that dried her mouth had no reason to it. She had walked that same footpath almost every day of her life, and had often passed groups of weavers. They tended to be garrulous, gathering together in the weaving shops if the weather was bad, and in the streets when it was fine.

But now ice trickled along her spine, and she knew all at once how a dog felt when the hairs on the back of its neck stood erect in times of danger.

She lowered her gaze to the path, afraid to look fully at the men in case they took it amiss.

Their shabby, broken shoes came into her view, strung across the way then, as she and Kerr approached steadily, shuffling back to make a path for them.

The fine hairs on the back of her neck prickled as he guided her through the middle of the group. It was foolish to feel so afraid in the streets she walked every day of her life, but she was, nevertheless. And she was grateful for the calm, reassuring strength of the man by her side.

Then they were by the group, the sense of some unspoken threat had faded behind them and she was able to lift her head again. Two children squabbling over a penny stepped aside to let them pass, a stout matron was helped from a carriage and waddled into a shop doorway, a thin, dry-looking merchant nodded to Kerr as he went by, and raised his hat to Rowena. Paisley was back to itself once again.

'Don't blame these poor souls,' Kerr said. 'They merely resent your fine clothes and your air of well-being. And why shouldn't they, when it's harder and harder to keep a family alive these days?'

She remembered Maxwell's thinly-veiled warning to him over the dinner-table in Carriagehill.

'If they should take the law into their own hands, would you join them?'

'You'd expect me to stay aloof — after the fiery speeches I've heard you make?'

'I think you've too much to lose.'

He sighed. She looked up to see that his face, beneath the

brim of the tall beaver hat he wore, was all planes and angles.

'Aye, you're right. I've other concerns on my mind, and my family to look to. I can't speak for Philip, though. There's to be a meeting soon, at Meikleriggs Moor. Had you heard?'

'The whole town's been ringing with it. Mister Bain thinks it should be forbidden.'

'He would,' Kerr said dryly. 'Him and all the other employers and land-owners. But they'll not dare to make such a move, for it would infuriate just about every working man in the town. Philip's of a mind to go. I'm hoping to persuade him against it, for he's spoiling for trouble.'

She thought of the resentment in Philip Fraser's eyes, the bitterness in his voice as he had spoken out in Alison's kitchen earlier, before his mother's collapse. 'He's filled with hatred.'

'Can you blame the lad?' asked Philip's brother. 'If he'd not been won over by the promise of a fine uniform and a grand life as a soldier he'd have the full use of all his limbs today.'

There was bitterness in his own voice. 'And what did the country he fought for do to show its gratitude? It sent him back home, only half a man, to live as best he may — on some menial work in the mill, or on charity, if he couldn't find anyone to offer him employment. It's only generals that gain acclaim and fortune when battles are won, for all that it's men such as Philip who do their fighting for them.'

'I think Ibby wants to marry him.' Although she and Ibby were as close as sisters the little maid's fierce devotion to Philip was something that Rowena had never been able to understand.

'Does she now? Then he's fortunate, for Ibby's a good wee soul, and loyal too. But how can Philip hope to support a wife on what he earns in the mill stores? D'you see how it is for young men like him, unable to afford the homes and families they crave, and frustrated almost beyond bearing? If he's got marriage on his mind it's little wonder that he's eager to see changes made in the way this country's run.'

But Rowena was no longer listening. She had stopped, her eyes fixed on Neil, who was standing at a shop doorway several yards away. He hadn't noticed her; his head was bent over Etta Brodie, and all his attention given to her.

'Did you not know?' Kerr, too, had seen the other two. 'He's with her often these days — scarcely away from the school-room when she's there, and out walking with her most evenings. Thon rich shawl-man's daughter doesn't seem to please him near as much as the school-mistress.'

It was Etta who looked up first and saw them. Sudden colour rose to her face in two bright spots over her cheekbones. She almost snatched a small bundle of books from Neil, bobbed a frightened half-curtsey in Rowena's direction, and ducked into the shop, out of sight.

Neil's face was a rich mixture of expressions; surprise at Etta's sudden disappearance, confusion and embarrassment when he turned and saw his sister, then haughty disapproval as he saw how Kerr's hand was cupped about her elbow.

In a few long strides he was with them. 'Rowena, have you no sense, walking about the streets when they're filled with mal-contents?'

'Your sister's quite safe, I assure you,' Kerr's voice was cool. 'I was escorting her home.'

'Good of you,' Neil said ungraciously. 'But now that I'm here I can escort her myself.'

Kerr's hand left Rowena's arm and he stepped back, lifting his hat to her with a formal gesture. 'Your servant, Mistress Rowena.' Then he nodded briefly, coldly, to Neil.

As they separated, he returning to the shop, she going back to Carriagehill with Neil's hand locked firmly about her arm almost as though she was a prisoner, her brother asked, 'What possessed you to encourage Kerr Fraser to escort you through the streets like that? He's seeking every opportunity he can find to visit Carriagehill and court the old man's attention.'

She tried to twitch her arm free, and couldn't, so she stepped out, forcing him to lengthen his own strides. 'Nonsense, Neil! Kerr has no need to resort to such trickery!'

'P'raps it's your own attention he seeks, then. That would be another way of making certain of his place in the mill — marry-ing with the daughter of the house.'

'I'm not the daughter of the house — I'm the daughter of one of the mill-workers, and you're his son.'

'Not any more! I can't understand why you're so set on

lowering yourself, and me into the bargain,' he almost hissed as they hurried along. 'Let me tell you this, my lady — you can find a better match than Kerr Fraser, and I'll see to it that you do!'

Anger almost choked her. She stopped and faced him, heedless of the other people using the path. 'Neil Lindsay, are your wits addled? Can two people not walk together along a public footpath without you getting stupid notions about them into your head?'

Two girls squeezing past them caught the last words, and stared and giggled. Neil, his face red, retained his hold on her arm and bustled her forward again.

'Don't turn yourself — and me — into a public exhibition! I'm just warning you to watch out for him. He's not the right man for you.'

'He was only escorting me home — just as you were escorting Etta Brodie.'

A sidelong glance showed that his flush had deepened to fiery red. 'I w — wasn't escorting her.' In his embarrassment he developed a slight stammer. 'We m — merely met and talked about — about the school-room.'

'Indeed?'

'I don't care for your tone, Rowena. Your trouble,' Neil quickly regained control, and his voice took on a note of maddening male superiority, 'is that you're too impetuous. You know very little about life.'

'I know that it's not all to be found in howffs and gambling houses and — and the mill school-room!' she snapped, and marched ahead of him, so angry that she bore down on another group of men idling on the footpath and walked straight through the middle of them, towing Neil with her, without turning a hair.

XI

The carriage was too small, and it was high time that Fergus bought a new, larger one. Sarah voiced her opinion several times as the four of them, the two young Lindsays and the two elderly Bains, made the journey from their Carriagehill home to the Saracen's Head Inn at the Cross.

'There's no sense in spending good silver on a large carriage, since it's seldom enough that the four of us have to travel together,' Fergus finally pointed out, goaded into speech by his wife's complaints.

'If we had a larger carriage we could use it to travel to Helensburgh, instead of having to rely on public transport,' she retorted. 'Bumpy coaches, not knowing who your neighbour might be — and I'll swear to it that I had a flea-bite on my arm the last time I travelled there.'

'No flea would dare to bite you, Sarah,' her husband told her, and she snapped a furious look across the small space to where he sat beside Neil.

'Quite apart from the fact that our friends must think we're either poor or miserly, my clothes are getting quite crushed in this small space.' Her pudgy, jewelled fingers fussed over her gown, a magnificent creation of oyster satin with an overdress of finest black lace.

Rowena, sharing the narrow carriage seat with her foster mother, tried to edge further away to make more room, although Sarah had already usurped at least half of the available space. Opposite her, Neil stared at a spot somewhere above her head, his thoughts elsewhere. He, like Fergus, had made an attempt to avoid this gathering that Maxwell King had decided to hold, but Sarah had refused to listen to either of them.

'D'you realise that in all the time we've known Maxwell, in all the years he's been our friend, he has never before held a grand gathering like this?' she had pointed out, and insisted on hurrying Rowena, who was well satisfied with her blue silk gown with the pine pattern, off to the dressmaker's to have a new dress made for the occasion.

The inn, on that fine early July evening, was a glitter of candle-light and colour that spilled from the windows and the open doorway as the carriage, now in line with many others, stopped to allow them to descend. Maxwell, handsome and elegant in plum-coloured velvet, was waiting to hand the ladies down himself and escort the Bain party into the inn.

A servant hurried forward to take their wraps; as Rowena's fur-trimmed pelisse was whisked deftly but deferentially from her shoulders her host's dark eyes slid with open approval over her new white silk gown. The bodice was cut square, and a little lower than Sarah thought suitable for her ward, although her own gown, as usual, showed far more cleavage than Rowena's. Silver and gold thread embroidery trimmed the neckline and the short puffed sleeves, and also decorated the bodice, which was artfully shaped to make the most of its wearer's slender waist and high young breasts.

Sky-blue ribbons, matching the sash about Rowena's waist, decorated the full skirt, which was gathered up near the hem to reveal a lace-edged sky blue petticoat.

'You look − charming,' Maxwell murmured to her as he led the party into the main hall, where a group of musicians played, and people were already dancing. 'But surely such a jewel deserves, herself, to be jewelled.'

She had noticed the faint frown as his gaze rested for just a second on her unadorned throat. 'I never wear jewellery, Mister King. I have none of my own, other than my cameo brooch − and never felt the need to possess any,' she added, half-defensively.

Then they were in the hall; all about them there was a sea of people, their voices and laughter rising to fill the air.

Whenever his duties as host permitted Maxwell was with Fergus's party, flattering Sarah skilfully, yet scarcely leaving Rowena's side.

'You have a natural feeling for the music,' he told her as he led her through a dance. She smiled radiantly at him.

'I love dancing. I took lessons from Mister Telford in

Causewayside Street for several years, and once or twice Neil took me to The Rooms — only Mistress Bain forbade that when those wicked pamphlets were circulated.'

'The Rooms' had been the local name for a series of assemblies held two winters before. They had proved to be very popular with the town's younger members, but when an attempt was made to bring them back the following winter a series of pamphlets, published under an assumed name by a divinity student who strongly disapproved of dancing, and accusing those who took part, particularly the young ladies, of being immoral, caused a storm in the town. Sarah had at once forbidden Neil and Rowena to attend the assemblies.

Rowena had missed those pleasant evenings. Now, dancing with a man who proved to be an excellent partner despite his years, she began to enjoy herself. When he had to leave her to attend to his duties, others came to take his place and claim her hand. The first two hours flew by.

She had no idea that Kerr was one of the guests until he suddenly appeared before her in a quiet window-recess where she had gone to rest between dances.

'May I—?' He held out his hands, and she rose at once and took them, to be drawn once again onto the dance floor.

'I didn't know you were here.'

'I arrived a good hour since, but you were busily engaged dancing with our host.'

'Not for a whole hour!'

'No,' he agreed blandly. 'But after that there was someone else, and then some other man, and then our host again. Then I was drawn into a side room to talk business with some gentlemen, and when I came out you were with our host once more, and then—'

'I like dancing.'

'So I realised.'

They circled, parted, came back together, joined hands once again. He was wearing the green coat she remembered from the dinner party, the first time they met after he came back to Paisley.

Again they parted, then rejoined each other as the dancers patterned their way round the floor. 'You look lovely tonight,

Rowena,' he said with a simple straightforwardness that meant more to her than a thousand pretty speeches from any other man.

Dazzled by a sudden surge of happiness, she put a hand to her smooth, warm throat. 'But I have no jewellery,' she said, and at once thought that it was one of the most stupid remarks she had ever made.

'Such a jewel deserves, herself, to be jewelled—' The words had tripped easily, prettily, from Maxwell's tongue. But Kerr, his eyes touching on her ear-lobes, her throat, her fingers, merely said, 'Jewels are all very well for plain women. You don't need them.'

When the music ended he led her back to the window recess and seated himself beside her.

'Or perhaps you'd rather go back to Mistress Bain?' he suggested, and she shook her head.

Summer dusk had given way to darkness since the dance began. When she turned away from the crowded room and tried to look out of the window all she could see, reflected in the glass, were the shadowy shapes of the dancers and nearer, as though they were just outside, herself and Kerr, her almost-naked shoulders gleaming, his thick hair forming a roughly-sketched halo about his head.

'Did you attend many dances while you were in England?'

'A few. They're as popular there as they are here.'

She turned back to face the room and for a moment they sat silently together, watching the people dancing past their little niche. Neil came by with Moira MacKenzie, and passed without seeing them. The girl was laughing and animated, happy to be with him; Neil himself still retained the gravity she had noticed in the coach.

'Etta Brodie's ill, did your brother tell you?' It wasn't the first time she had known Kerr to pick up her thoughts.

'He never speaks about her, to me or to the Bains. What's amiss with her?'

'Her lungs are bad. My mother's been going round to the house to lend a hand in the evenings, for Etta's own mother's not strong.'

There was a smattering of applause as the dance ended, then

another began and Maxwell came to claim Rowena and lead her onto the dance floor.

'Are you enjoying yourself?'

'Oh, indeed!' she assured him. 'I've never in my life seen so many folk gathered together under one roof − except in the kirk, of course.'

'I felt that it was high time I repaid all the hospitality that's been shown to me over the years. It's difficult for a man on his own to hold dinner parties − for all that I've got a good staff of servants. So I decided that this place would be more fitting—' He indicated the vast room where they danced, and the ante-rooms leading from it, where refreshments had been served. 'For the Scots enjoy nothing more than the space and the opportunity to dance.'

'I understand from Mistress Bain that your own house is large, and very fine.'

'But somewhat gloomy, and lacking a woman's touch. You must come and inspect it for yourself one day. I'll make a point of arranging it soon.'

He was right − the Scots did enjoy dancing. As the evening wore on and the guests began to settle in, the more formal English dances gradually gave way to strathspeys and reels; the music got faster, the floor bounced and creaked to the thump of feet, the high ceiling caught and threw back the cries of the dancers as Paisley's sedate and well-to-do citizens began to enjoy themselves in earnest.

Maxwell, shrugging his shoulders helplessly, finally gave up and went to sit beside Fergus, who was watching the dancers with a broad grin on his face, reliving his own youth. Even Neil lost his air of pre-occupation and joined in with enthusiasm.

Rowena wove her way along a row of people, her feet twinkling in time to the quick beat of the music as she linked arms with first one and then another and then a third, weaving her way down the line, twisting in and out as deftly and rapidly as a needle flashing through material. Kerr was waiting for her; they linked arms, spun, separated, then joined outstretched hands and danced back up between two long lines of people. He laughed down at her, flushed and happy and heart-touchingly youthful now that he was free of his everyday problems. Her hands were lost in his, her feet scarcely touched the floor.

Everything – her unhappiness about her father, the threat of revolution that hung over the town that summer like a cloud, her concern over Neil – vanished as she danced with her hands in Kerr's.

She wished, as she laughed back at him, that this moment could go on for always, and never, never stop.

*

Burn Row, where Etta Brodie lived with her parents, was a collection of tiny old cottages not far from Gordon's Loan. It got its name from the Espedair Burn, which wound round Saucel Hill to discharge itself into the river just beyond the cottages. Burn Row was just off Orchard Street, on land where, centuries before, the monks of the great Abbey had grown their fruit and vegetables. Now the only vegetation growing in the area was tough grass that forced itself up between the cobbles, and dank moss found in clumps on the slimy, broken-down outer walls of the little houses.

Rowena hesitated outside Etta's door for a moment, looking up and down the narrow lane. Children, some of them too young to walk, played on the footpaths, in and out of the stagnant puddles that always seemed to be present in old lanes like Burn Row, even in the hottest summer. Women gossiping on their doorsteps had stopped to stare at her as she passed, their eyes almost devouring her clothes and the basket she carried.

Two of them, an old crone twisted by rheumatism until she resembled an ancient tree, and a fat young woman with a headful of tangled black hair, even suspended their foul-mouthed shouting match to watch her as she knocked on the door.

It opened slowly, reluctantly, and an old man peered out at her.

'Yes?' His eyes, painfully inflamed, looked her up and down. When she explained that she had come to visit the sick girl she said nothing, but stared. She said it again, on a louder note, well aware that the listening women would now be able to hear her, and still he gaped dumbly. Then all at once a scrawny hand was clamped on his shoulder and he disappeared as though twitched out of the way. A woman every bit as old and thin and bent took his place and pulled the door wide to let Rowena in.

'Come in, mistress. It's good of you to come enquiring after our poor lassie.'

Inside, the house was dark and small-roomed, old and cheerless and damp, as though the close proximity of Espedair Burn and the River Cart had overcome the efforts of plaster and wood and stone to keep them out. Etta lay in the wall-bed in the kitchen, her brilliant green eyes and flushed cheeks giving clownish patches of colour to her white little face.

She was propped on one elbow, watching the door eagerly. When her mother stepped aside and Rowena came into view, the sick girl's smile faded, and she lay back on her stained pillow, her fingers plucking at the ragged blanket that covered her.

'Mistress Row—' Her voice was hoarse, and the effort to speak set her coughing. Her mother ran to fill a cup with water, and the girl took it and sipped at it.

The old man had gone to sit by the range as though disinterested in what was going on. Watching him, Rowena was reminded of her own father's behaviour when she visited Common Loan. She put her basket on the table and began to unpack its contents.

'I brought some things for Etta—' Diffidently, suddenly afraid that her gesture of friendship might offend the little family, she laid food, some fruit, a warm shawl and two of her own favourite books on the table. The old woman watched avidly, eyes bright.

'Bless you, mistress. You'll take some tea?' She went across the worn, uneven floor to the range and swung the big kettle, suspended from an iron 'swee' for easy movement, across until it was above the fire.

Etta's coughing fit had subsided. Rowena took the cup from her and put it aside as the girl wiped her mouth with a rag that lay near her hand for the purpose.

'Did Neil ask you to come?'

'Yes,' Rowena lied, seeing the eager hope in the girl's eyes. Etta gave her a radiant smile.

'He's been so kind – sending money, and assuring me that I'll not lose my place in the school-room because of being ill.' Then the smile faltered slightly. 'I'd hoped – I mean, I'd wondered if – but I expect he's very busy in the counting house.'

'Yes, he is.' A wave of compassion swept over Rowena as she looked at the girl, ravaged by the lung disease that was all too common in the town. 'Has the physician been to see you yet?'

Etta began to speak, then caught up the rag and pressed it to her lips as another bout of coughing seized her.

'Aye, he's been here.' Her mother spoke for her, bringing Rowena a cup half-filled with strong tea. 'He's left medicines, and word that she's to rest until he says she's able to be about her duties again.'

The tea tasted bitter. Rowena sipped at it, forcing each tiny mouthful down her throat. Her stomach rebelled, but she knew full well how difficult it must be for this little family, dependent on Etta's earnings at the mill, to afford such luxuries as tea, and how proud old Mistress Brodie must feel at being able to offer it to her visitor. Not one drop must be wasted.

'Did he not suggest that Etta should be taken to the House of Recovery until she was better?'

Etta, still trying to overcome her coughing fit, didn't hear her. The old man turned and gave her a brief, almost contemptuous glance before going back to his study of the range and the thin plume of steam floating steadily from the kettle's spout to add its own contribution to the room's general dampness.

'He did,' Etta's mother, holding the cup of water in readiness for her daughter, was unperturbed by the question. 'But bless you, mistress, the folk there have already sent our other four bairns to their graves, after they were taken in with bad lungs. We're not minded to let them kill the only one left to us.'

*

She followed Neil to his room after dinner that night.

'I called on Etta Brodie today.'

His dark head came up swiftly at mention of the girl's name; for just a moment, before he got himself under control, his eyes sought hers hungrily, then he looked away with studied indifference. 'Did you?'

'I took some things that I thought the family might need. They live in a very poor cottage.'

He said nothing, staring out of the window at the flower beds below as though they were of great interest.

'Her mother told me that you've sent money to help them while Etta's ill.'

'She's a good worker.' Neil's voice was flat, without emotion.

'More than just a good worker, surely.' She waited, but he didn't reply. 'Neil, I know well enough that you're friends, you and Etta. There's no harm in it, for she's a fine lassie. It would mean a great deal to her if you'd just take a few minutes to go to Burn Row yourself and call on her. I'm sure—'

'Me – go to Burn Row?' Neil rounded on her, his eyes vivid blue in a face pale with anger. 'Call on a mill employee?' He choked out a scornful laugh. 'I leave that sort of thing to you, my dear sister! You're the one who delights in tripping in and out of cottages and shop kitchens – not me!'

'But Etta's more than an employee, surely.'

'She's an able schoolmistress – and I'm manager in the counting-house. There can be nothing more between us!'

'You're also the son of the store-man. If things had been different you'd have been living in a cottage yourself, and as like as not working in the store along with our father.'

For a moment she thought that he was going to leap across the room and strike her. He controlled himself with an effort and picked up his jacket.

'But things are different, Rowena, and don't you forget it. I'm the owner's foster-son. I have been for many years.' He forced the words between clenched jaws. 'Aunt Sarah gets vexed enough about your refusal to behave as you should. God knows what she'd say if I was foolish enough to follow your example.'

It was obvious that she wasn't going to change his mind. She opened the door quietly and left him to his own thoughts.

As she was stepping out into the upper hall Neil, staring out at the garden again, asked, in a low voice that she almost missed, 'How is she?'

'I think she's very ill,' Rowena said, and closed the door between them.

Neil left the house a few minutes later, and returned in the early hours of the morning. Rowena, who had been sitting in her room, waiting for him, crept along to his room after a few minutes, and found him spread-eagled over the bed, fully dressed and sound asleep. The room reeked of drink and stale smoke.

She covered him with a rug and went back to bed.

XII

As the day of the big meeting on Meikleriggs Moor drew near Sarah grew increasingly nervous.

She was convinced, despite Fergus's assurances to the contrary, that the working men and women who intended to go to the meeting would become inflamed by the political speeches, and would then descend on the town, robbing and looting — and worse.

'God save us, woman, you're talking of folk we see every day of our lives — folk who work in the mill, and walk by you in Paisley's streets, and attend the same kirk on Sundays, if it comes to that,' her husband protested. 'I'll not say I'm in favour of the meeting, and I'll admit that there are some who'll use it as an excuse for mischief, but most of them are honest, decent men who just want the London Parliament to heed their complaints.'

But Sarah wouldn't be re-assured. 'You can take your chance with them, then — I'm for Helensburgh,' she announced, and within forty-eight hours she and her housekeeper had gone rattling off in the public coach to the safety of the seaside town.

To Sarah's annoyance, nobody else would accompany her. Fergus wanted to stay near the mill, just in case there was trouble after the meeting; Neil was bound to attend to his work in the counting-house, and Rowena refused to leave the town just when something exciting was about to happen.

The fuss caused by Sarah's departure had scarcely had time

to die down when a letter for her was delivered by hand. Fergus opened it, then limped painfully into the drawing-room in search of Rowena.

'It seems that Maxwell King offered at some time to show you over his house. Now he's written to Sarah to suggest that the two of you take tea with him tomorrow afternoon.'

She took the letter and studied the clear, decisive handwriting. 'I'll write and explain that an acceptance must wait until Mistress Bain returns.'

'I see no reason why you shouldn't go,' said Fergus mildly.

'On my own? It wouldn't be seemly.'

'But, lassie, you're young enough to be Maxwell's—' Fergus Bain paused and took time to look at the girl standing before him. Pre-occupied with the mill and then with his own failing health he hadn't noticed the years hurrying past. The shy, gawky little red-haired girl who had come to his house after the canal basin disaster had given way, unnoticed by him, to a tall, slender, attractive young woman.

'But p'rhaps you're right at that. How old are you now?'

'Recently turned seventeen, sir.'

'Hhhmmmph. Well, I'm past wanting to take jaunts now, and anyway, I've seen Maxwell's house often enough. Neil can go with you. As I remember it, Maxwell has a fine stable he'll enjoy. It'll be an outing for you both.'

Maxwell King's residence, far enough from the town to be halfway to the village of Barrhead, was a square grey stone building, set well back from the road so that it could only be properly seen from its own gravelled driveway.

Sunlight reflected from big windows, turning the house into a vast diamond-studded brooch as the carriage Maxwell had sent for the young Lindsays came through the trees and they saw the house for the first time.

'He does himself well,' Neil commented admiringly, then the carriage stopped before the wide stone steps that led from the terrace before the house, and Maxwell himself was moving forward to meet them.

'Before we have tea, I must keep my promise to show you round the house,' he said to Rowena, then turned to Neil. 'If you'd prefer it, you can visit the stables and try out the new animal I've bought.'

Neil's boredom immediately lifted, and a servant was sent for, to show him to the stables. Then the tour began.

The house was larger than the Bains', and much more grand. At first, Rowena tried to maintain a polite, restrained interest, but there was so much to see and to exclaim over that she quickly gave up all pretence, and settled down to enjoy openly the beautiful, intricate wrought iron balusters, so much lighter and more graceful than wood, the ornamented cornices round the doors, the marble-topped table in the hall with its elaborate, gilded supports, the tapestry chairs, the clocks, the mirrors with their carved frames.

She marvelled over the superb chimney pieces in the main rooms, with paintings set into their carved cornices, the walls papered with pastoral scenes and floral garlands, the ornate ceilings and the parquetage floors in the dining room and drawing room, with inlaid patterns of differently coloured woods.

The floor of the big entrance hall was of coloured marble and the bedrooms were floored with polished oak.

'It's the most beautiful house I've ever seen!' she said in awe as they returned to the entrance hall.

'But altogether too gloomy, altogether too—' the owner of the house cast a look around '—too formal. It's no longer a home. Would you care to see the garden?'

They went along the terrace, round the corner to the side of the house, and down steps to the lawn. This in turn led to a small rose-garden, heavy with scent, the paved paths sprinkled with fallen crimson and pink and white yellow petals.

'When I first came to Paisley – when I was Fergus's partner in the mill – my bride was with me.' Maxwell picked a full-blown peach-coloured rose and twirled it absently in his fingers as he talked.

'She fell in love with this house, and so I bought it for her as soon as I could afford it. We planned to fill it with children, but unfortunately the Fates decided otherwise. In the years since her death I've been too pre-occupied with business to give much thought to the house. The servants take care of it well enough, but—' He let the sentence drift away on the rose-scented air, then smiled down at her.

'Today, through your eyes and your pleasure in it, I saw it all anew. And I saw, too, that it sorely needs a mistress again.'

His eyes held hers. The air was suddenly still, the smell of the roses a little too cloying.

'I'm sure that there are many ladies who would be pleased to be mistress of such a fine house—' she said lamely, then hurried on, 'Which way is it to the stables? It must be time to fetch Neil, if we're to have tea before we go back to Carriagehill.'

To her relief he nodded, and led the way back across the lawn and round to the courtyard at the rear of the house, where her brother stood talking to a groom.

Neil's enthusiasm for the horse he had just ridden swept the conversation along as they took tea in the large drawing room.

At Maxwell's request, Rowena nervously took charge of the silver tea-service; whenever she glanced up, she saw his eyes fixed on her, his mouth curved in a faint smile as though he approved of the sight of her playing hostess in his home.

Inevitably, the talk turned to the meeting to be held on the following day.

'I trust you'll stay indoors, where you're safe, Miss Rowena,' Maxwell accepted his re-filled cup from her.

'I expect I must, for Mister Bain's peace of mind. But I can't think that there'll be trouble, knowing the Paisley folk.'

'Let the ordinary people get together and you have a herd of animals,' Maxwell said crisply, and she felt her face grow stiff with resentment. 'There's no knowing what they might get up to once they're roused.'

Then, as though he noticed her sudden cool silence, he turned the conversation to other, less controversial matters.

'I'd like to think,' Neil said dreamily as they drove away an hour later, 'that one day I'd own a place as grand as that one.'

Then, as she said nothing, he prompted, 'Wouldn't you?'

'It's very lovely — but perhaps it's too large.'

'Nonsense — the man can well afford the servants needed to run such a house. I can't think why he never married again — pretty well any woman would give all she possessed to be mistress

of such a place. It's more grand than the MacKenzies' house —
and old man MacKenzie has plenty of money.'

'Is that all that matters to you, Neil — money?'

'What else is there?' her brother asked.

'A lot of things.' A picture of Etta Brodie, frail and beautiful,
rose before her eyes. 'Respect, for one. Love, for another.'

'I respect money — and as for love, it's an emotion that few of
us can afford to pamper ourselves with.'

Then he chuckled. 'D'you know what I think? If you set your
mind to it, you could marry Maxwell King and gain that house
of his yourself. I saw the way he watched you when you were
busying yourself about the tea-table.'

The carriage turned a corner, and a cool breeze caused a shiver
to run along Rowena's spine. 'Maxwell King's too old for me.'

'He's a fine-looking man, with years of life in him, I'd say.
And it's time you were thinking of marriage, surely.'

Then his voice sharpened and he leaned forward to get a
better look at her face beneath the brim of her bonnet. 'You're
not running away with foolish thoughts about someone like Kerr
Fraser, are you? You can do better for yourself than that!'

'Kerr's the mill manager!'

'Only because the old man's got a soft spot for him. We've still
to find out if he's as good as he thinks he is. Are you, Rowena?
Are you getting a fondness for him? If so, I'm warning you that
I'll not have it! I'll not have my sister marrying beneath her!'

'Have your senses left you altogether?' Mindful of the coachman, she kept her voice low. 'We're not gentry, Neil.'

'But we were raised by gentry. We've got used to money, you
and me. And the only way we can keep it is by marrying well.
Moira MacKenzie for me, as like as not, and for you — well, you
could do worse than settle for Maxwell King.'

The sheer stupidity of his argument was almost amusing.
That thought made it possible to swallow her anger and say,
sweetly 'If we're home in time, I must call in at Burn Row and
see how Etta is.'

Neil's mouth closed with an almost audible snap. He sat back
in his corner of the carriage, scowling at the brilliantly flowered
hedgerows, and said nothing more until the carriage rolled to a
standstill outside the Bains' front door.

XIII

All roads led to Paisley on July 17th, the day of the meeting to call for reformation in Parliament.

As work ended at noon men and women came from the manufactories and the weaving shops to join the stream of people already making their way to Meikleriggs Moor from Glasgow and Neilston, Barrhead and Renfrew, Kilbarchan and Elderslie.

Under the warm sun they trudged, some filled with hope, some with determination, others plagued by a fierce desperate anger, a thirst that would not be satisfied until the wrongs they felt their country was committing against them were righted.

Neil left early in the morning for Glasgow, where he had work to do on Watson and Bain's behalf. Fergus satisfied himself that everything was in order in the house, then went off in the gig to the mill, where he intended to stay until the meeting was over and the people dispersed back to their homes.

'The special constables have been called out — and if those who say that thousands'll be making their way to the meeting are right, there could be trouble in the streets afterwards when they encounter the constables,' he prophesied before he left the house. 'I must keep a watchful eye on the mill. You'd best stay indoors, Rowena, and make certain that the servants do the same. I've no wish to see any member of my household caught up in whatever may happen. Keep out of the way, and let the folk thrash out their own problems as best they may, that's my advice.'

Throughout the morning people poured past the big gates at the end of the driveway, most of them coming in from the weaving villages of Barrhead and Neilston to attend the meeting. But by the time the speeches were due to start the place was almost deserted, and eerily silent.

Rowena, too restless to stay indoors all day, slipped out and went to Gordon's Loan, taking Ibby for company. They had time to spend an hour or more with Alison and be home long before the meeting broke up and the people began to return.

As they hurried through the empty streets she fancied she heard, now and then, the roar of thousands of voices, and tried to imagine what was happening on the Moor. What were the speakers saying? What was it like to be part of a great army of people bent on forcing dramatic changes in the ways of their world?

The shop was closed. 'Lest the windows get smashed, on a day like this,' Ibby said, nodding sagely.

The two girls went through the side passageway and let themselves in at the door. Alison, sitting in her favourite chair, didn't move as they entered. Rowena took one look at the older woman's face, and sent Ibby running to fetch a physician.

'She's worn out, heart and body,' he said an hour later, when the three of them had settled Alison Fraser in the kitchen wallbed. 'There's little any of us can do for her, except make her as comfortable as possible. Where are her sons?' Then he answered his own question. 'At the Moor, no doubt. Let me know if there's any change.'

He went, and Rowena, without much hope, sent a barefoot boy from the street to find Kerr and Philip and bring them home. Then she and Ibby watched over Alison, who lay with her eyes closed and her face strangely smooth and remote.

It was as though, having given every minute of her life so far to others, she had run out of anything else to give, and had withdrawn with frightening suddenness.

Time dragged by, and still Kerr and Philip didn't come home. As word of Alison Fraser's sudden illness spread, women from the neighbourhood arrived to take up the age-old vigil with the dying, and the little house adopted a new and frightening solemnity, as though the very walls knew what was about to happen.

Finally, unable to bear the atmosphere any longer, Rowena stood up and reached for her shawl.

'The meeting must be over by now. I'm going to find Kerr.'

'You'd be well advised to bide where you are,' an old woman told her. 'You're safer in than out today.'

But she had to get away from the sight of Alison Fraser's dying.

'I'm coming with you,' Ibby said, adding, as Rowena gave her a grateful look, 'If anything should happen to you the master'll have my skin. We might as well die out in the streets together, if that's God's wish.'

Causewayside Street was filling with people, most of them marching down the middle of the thoroughfare in clusters, talking and laughing loudly, flushed with excitement, impeding the carts and carriages and horse-riders. Some brandished flags, others carried branches or pieces ripped from fences as they passed. Most of them were bright-eyed and belligerent, drunk with the sun and the speeches, ready for trouble.

Rowena, with Ibby's bony fingers clutching her wrist, stopped at the corner of Gordon's Loan and Causewayside Street, wondering which way to go in her search for Kerr and Philip.

'The specials are at the Cross!' An old man, literally spitting out the words in his excitement, made up her mind for her. 'They've seized the Glasgow men's flags!'

The girls were almost swept aside in the rush towards St Mirren's Street and the Cross, where the fighting the crowd was spoiling for had already broken out. The road was clear for a moment; Rowena and Ibby hurried across it and ran along Common Lane, past Ewan Lindsay's house, and up Wardrop Street. Kerr would avoid the mêlée at the Cross, Rowena thought as they ran. He and Philip would no doubt come home down Storrie Street, and they would meet with them somewhere along the way.

She and Ibby crossed George Street, turned the corner into Storrie Street, and stopped, appalled, as a tide of men and women swept down the hill towards them, banners waving above their heads.

They hesitated for only a moment, but it was a moment too long. As they turned to go back more people poured along George Street.

Desperately, convinced that if the crowd swept down on them they would be carried all the way to the Cross, and into the fighting, Rowena scrambled for the pitifully shallow safety of a doorway, dragging Ibby after her. They pressed themselves back against the wooden panels; then the mob, chanting and shouting, laughing and cursing, was sweeping past, filling the street from wall to wall, so tightly packed that there was scarcely an inch of ground uncovered.

The noise was deafening. Rowena wanted to cover her ears, but both hands were needed to cling to the door-frame. Faces whirled by, banners and sticks flailed the air, sometimes only a few inches from her face. The people were passing in their hundreds, a never-ending procession.

A whirling stick caught the fringe of her good Paisley shawl and dragged it from around her shoulders. Ibby snatched at it and almost toppled from the worn doorstep. Rowena only just managed to catch the maid's arm and pull her back to safety.

'Your bonny shawl!'

'Let it go!' It had been a great favourite, that shawl, but she watched it pass out of sight, flourished triumphantly aloft on the stick's point, without a pang. As long as she and Ibby were safe nothing else mattered.

It seemed to take hours before the crowd began to thin out. Cramped with the effort of clinging to the narrow step, shivering with a mixture of fear and excitement, Rowena finally began to sense that she and the maid were no longer threatened by the press of bodies. The folk passing them had room to walk comfortably; then the numbers dwindled to knots of two and three, and finally there were the stragglers, those who lagged behind because they were merely there to spectate, those who were busily engaged in talking, and those who were too old or too young or too infirm to keep up with the main body of the mob.

'Philip!' Ibby suddenly launched herself from the doorway, almost knocking Rowena over. She steadied herself in time to see the little maid grab at Philip Fraser's sleeve as he walked down the middle of the street.

Kerr, Rowena saw with a leap of joy, had a grip of Philip's other arm, arguing with him; the lame man, held on both sides now, twisted and turned in an effort to free himself.

'Leave me be — I'm going to the Cross, I tell you!'

'To get yourself taken by the militia, and hurt in the process?' Kerr demanded angrily. 'Don't be a fool, man!'

Then his eyes, as grey today as storm-clouds coming in over the braes behind Paisley, widened as Rowena left the doorway and ran into the roadway, almost losing her balance as she caught her foot on a branch someone had dropped. She pulled free and heard the hem of her dove-grey gown with the yellow flowers tearing.

'What are you doing out in the streets on a day like this?' he wanted to know, as sharply as if she belonged to him.

Philip, taking advantage of his brother's temporary lapse, pulled away from him and limped to the other side of the road, towing Ibby with him. He caught hold of a piece of fencing and twisted at it, dragging it free with ease.

'Your mother's poorly. She — needs you!' Dust caught at the back of Rowena's throat and set her coughing as soon as she began to speak.

Kerr didn't waste time on questions. 'Philip, we're wanted at the house!'

Philip hoisted the stick, his mouth writhing. 'Later!'

'Now!'

Kerr snatched at the weapon. His brother clung to it, and the two of them wrestled. One end, jagged where it had been wrenched free, struck Kerr in the face before, using his superior strength, he managed to force the stick from Philip's hands.

Cursing, the younger man, Ibby still clinging to his arm like a physician's leech, threw himself at his brother. Kerr tossed the stick aside and dealt Philip a swinging open-handed blow to the side of the head that sent him reeling. He lost his footing, slipped, and tumbled into the gutter.

Ibby, suddenly a virago, released him and flew at Kerr, tears sparkling on her cheeks, her fingers crooked into claws. He fended her off easily, passed her to Rowena with a curt 'See to her!' and went to drag his brother to his feet.

Rowena held Ibby back when the girl would have launched herself at his broad back once more.

'Ibby — think on poor Mistress Fraser!'

The girl hesitated, then the fight drained out of her. Without another word she went back to Philip, now standing sullenly in

Kerr's grip, and took his free arm, murmuring something to him.

'You'll take up your quarrel with the militia another day, no doubt,' Kerr said grimly. 'For now, we're needed at home.'

He started off at a fast pace, almost carrying his brother. Ibby had to run to keep up with them both. Rowena, forgotten, picked up Kerr's hat, which had been knocked into the side of the road during the struggle, and followed along behind the other three.

Causewayside Street was quieter now that the bulk of the mob had passed by. Further along, at the Bank, they could see the backs of the people still trying to crowd up St Mirren's Street to the Cross. There was only one man hurrying away from the crowd, coming in their direction. As he neared them Rowena saw with a sinking heart that it was Neil.

It was too late to slip round the corner and out of sight. He came up to them, his naturally pale face almost grey, his eyes dark with anger.

'Are you quite mad, Rowena?' Then, without waiting for an answer, he swept on, 'I near lost my life when I was coming through the Cross! If it hadn't been for one of the militia the rabble would've had me over the bridge and into the river. By God, if I'd my way of it, it would be the gallows for half the scum and transportation for the rest!'

Philip made a move forward, an angry growl deep in his throat. Kerr's grip tightened on his arm.

'Both these ladies are in need of an escort home. Mebbe you'd be good enough to provide it.'

There was an air of quiet authority in his voice, despite his anxiety over his mother and the effort of controlling Philip. Rowena saw by Neil's face that he recognised and resented it.

'Did you have the impertinence to take my sister to that confounded meeting? If you have, Fraser, I'll see that you answer for it—'

Rowena stepped forward, standing between the two men. 'I've not been to the meeting — and if I had wished to go, I shouldn't have required permission, or an escort.'

Her brother's eyes travelled over her with growing disbelief. 'Where's your bonnet — and your shawl?'

She put a hand to her hair and discovered that her bonnet had gone.

'I must have lost them when Ibby and I were caught up in the crowd, before we met Mister Fraser and his brother.' She hoped to make it clear that they had been rescued by Kerr and Philip, rather than led astray by them.

Neil's gaze moved to the three standing at her back. His lip curled, and she suddenly realised what a sight they must make. Her hair was straggling round her face, her dress dusty and torn, and her hands stained with green slimy moss from the doorway where she and Ibby had sheltered.

Ibby was in as sorry a state as herself, and Philip's clothes were dirty from the gutter where he had fallen when Kerr hit him.

She turned to hand Kerr's hat back to him, and saw that his thick hair was tousled and dried blood marked his cheekbone where the stick had cut his face during the struggle.

'What a crowd of hooligans we must look,' she said with a shaky laugh. Kerr's eyes, as they lifted above her head to meet Neil's, were glass-clear with cold anger. The tension between the two men was so strong she could almost hear it thrumming like an over-stretched spring.

'Come on, Neil, we must get home before Mister Bain begins to worry.' She put a hand on his arm. 'Kerr, I trust your mother's—' The trite, formal words stuck in her throat as she thought of Alison Fraser as she had last seen her.

'I think you'd best go to her now,' she said instead. 'Ibby—' And she led Neil past the brothers without more ado, intent only on getting him away from Kerr.

Ibby loosed her fingers from Philip's arm, peeped up apologetically into his face; then, seeing nothing but sullen resentment, realising that at that moment he was scarcely aware of her presence, she trailed unhappily after the Lindsays.

XIV

Although she had come down in the world Alison Fraser had continued to worship at the High Kirk, near the big house her husband had taken her to as his bride. So it was to the High Kirk burial ground that her body was carried three days after the meeting at Meikleriggs Moor.

A long procession followed the coffin up the steep stony hill to the kirk gates. Alison's kindliness and courage had endeared her to many people, and they came together to see her laid to rest.

In the kirkyard Rowena stood beneath the dazzling blue July sky with Fergus Bain by her side. She would have liked to walk from the shop with the other mourners, but Fergus's legs were paining him badly, so they had arrived by carriage, and were there slightly ahead of those who had come on foot.

Paisley was only just calming down after days and nights of rioting. On that first evening, as the crowds made their way home from the meeting, there had been violent clashes between the militia and the weavers. Windows in the Council Chambers and in the homes of some of the less popular employers had been smashed. The cavalry had finally been sent for and had managed to drive the folk back to their homes.

On the following evening, the Sabbath, while Kerr and Philip mourned their mother, reinforcements swarmed in from surrounding villages and the rioting started again, centred this time in Storrie Street, where railings torn from the area in front of the Methodist Church were used against the soldiers when they charged the crowd.

It was cruel, Rowena thought as the mourners took their places by the open grave, that the end of Alison's life should have been marred by such troubled events.

She looked across at Kerr, who stared down into the gaping space waiting to receive his mother's body. His face was set and expressionless. Philip was close by his side, lips tightened to a thin line, tear-filled hazel eyes glittering like jewels in a white mask of a face.

Once, during the minister's recitation of his mother's virtues, Kerr raised his head and looked directly at Rowena. Their eyes met and held; he smiled at her, the ghost of a smile that barely touched his eyes or his mouth, then he looked back down at the coffin.

Watching him when the burial was over, Alison was laid to her final rest, and the mourners were taking their leave, she thought of the lad who had gazed at her mother adoringly on a long-ago Martinmas Day, and minutes later dragged Rowena herself from the water in the canal basin.

Years later, returned to Paisley from his travels, he had become a confident young man, eager and willing to shoulder his new responsibilities at the mill.

And now he had changed yet again. The past few days of grieving had brought him to full maturity. In a way, he had become a stranger once more, and yet—

With a sense of shock that almost made her cry out, Rowena realised the subtle way in which her own feelings towards him had changed during those years. Childish admiration had slipped into warm friendship, and that, in its turn, had altered as surely and as swiftly as Kerr himself had altered.

She loved him. She wanted no other man — only him. She loved him, loved him — the phrase sang in her head, over and over again, and she almost went to him there and then, in the graveyard, before all the people, to put her arms about him and share in his suffering.

But such conduct, no matter how much she might desire it, was not seemly. So she walked by Fergus's side, and permitted Kerr to take her finger-tips into his icy clasp for a brief moment, and looked up into his face, and saw that in this moment of deep grief it was closed, even to her.

Then she touched Philip's hand, felt it shrink from contact with her fingers, saw the chill in his eyes, dry now that he had managed to force the weak tears back.

Fergus laid his hand on her arm, and she obediently went

with him, leaving the brothers together to greet the rest of the people who had come to see Alison buried.

As they walked slowly back to the carriage, Fergus's arm in hers, he said, 'I'm going to Helensburgh tomorrow. All this business—' he waved a hand vaguely, encompassing the grave-yard behind them and the town at the foot of the hill where the High Church stood; she had no way of knowing whether he referred to the riots, or Alison Fraser's death, or a combination of the two events '– has wearied me. I've no heart for anything. It's best that I go away for a while. Neil and young Fraser can manage well enough at the mill, I dare say, and the servants'll look after the two of you—'

But she had recently been giving thought to her own situation. 'I can't stay under your roof for the rest of my life.'

'My dear girl,' he was genuinely surprised. 'Nobody expects you to. No doubt you'll marry, in due course.'

'I'm not speaking of marriage.' Her voice was tinged with irritation. Why must men divide womankind into two categories – servants or wives, depending on their station in life? 'I must find some way to earn my living.'

'But you've no need to seek employment.'

'Indeed I have. If my mother hadn't died I'd have been working long since – probably in your mill. I'm not your daughter – I've no call on your kindness now that I'm grown.'

'So—' Fergus Bain said on a long pensive note. 'Where will you live – with your father and his wife?'

'No, I must find lodgings.'

'And work in the mill.'

She thought of the vast hot rooms, smelling of oil and cloudy with cotton fibres and noisy with the clacking of the machines. 'Others have to do it.'

After a moment's thought he said, 'Since my wife took Mistress Cochrane to Helensburgh with her the running of the house has fallen on your shoulders. Would it ease your independent spirit if I asked you to stay on under my roof as housekeeper?'

'What will Mistress Bain say to that?'

'I'm entitled to make my own arrangements. Or would you as soon apply for a place in the mill, or in a shop?'

There was gentle irony in his voice, but when she looked up

swiftly his face was carefully solemn. She felt a sudden rush of warmth for this gruff man.

'I'd be pleased to see to your house for you.'

They had reached the carriage. As William, the coachman, came forward to assist him she heard Fergus say quietly, 'I could wish Neil had more of your spirit.'

*

She took her new responsibilities as housekeeper very seriously. The servants had been accepting her orders without complaint ever since Sarah deserted them for the new house in Helensburgh, but they were surprised to find that now Rowena worked along with them.

'It isn't right!' Ibby wailed as she scuttled round a great chest of drawers on her knees, polishing cloth active, and found Rowena vigorously burnishing the other side. 'Mistress Bain'd never do such a thing!'

'Mistress Bain's a lady.'

'And what are you then?' Ibby wanted to know, sitting back on her heels and pushing lank hair from her eyes.

'A Paisley lass, the same as you — and I'm earning my keep, same as you. Now stop squawking and get on with it!'

Neil disapproved, as she knew he would, but she trapped her tongue between her teeth and let him rail on at her until he gave up and left her to her own devices, announcing that he only hoped that she wouldn't embarrass him should guests call.

'I'd scarce meet them in the drawing room with a blacking brush in one hand and a flat iron in the other,' she pointed out.

'I wish I could be certain of that,' he said darkly.

Rowena baked and scrubbed, polished and sewed, planned meals and dealt with the tradesmen, and tackled each day with new vigour.

There were few callers, since it was widely known that Sarah was away from home. Those who drove up to the door did so mainly because they were curious to see how the house was being run in the absence of both mistress and master.

They were met with courtesy and hospitality, and went away remarking to each other that Rowena Lindsay had quite become the young lady, a credit to dear Sarah's charitable generosity.

Neil had little to complain about when Mistress MacKenzie and her daughter Moira numbered themselves among the unexpected callers. As good fortune would have it Rowena, who was baking, was warned of their arrival by Ibby, who whirled into the kitchen, her face gleaming like a rosy apple, gasping out that she had seen the MacKenzie carriage on the road, and it looked to be making for that very house.

By the time the ladies had alighted Rowena had whipped off her apron, washed the flour from her hands, tidied her hair, and arrived on the doorstep to meet them. The drawing room, turned out that very morning by herself and Ibby, was immaculate.

Neil, who came home to find a pleasant little tea party in progress, shot his sister a grateful look as the two of them waved the guests off.

'You know—' Rowena said thoughtfully as they went back into the house. 'Moira MacKenzie's nicer than I first thought. She's got a good head on her shoulders, and a nice gentle nature.'

'Of course she has!' he snapped huffily.

'And she has a real fondness for you. Are you still minded to marry with her?'

'Probably,' he said briefly, and went upstairs to his room.

She watched him go, satisfaction with the way the visit had gone giving way to the worries that always nagged at her when she thought of her brother. Etta Brodie had recovered sufficiently enough to take up her duties in the mill school-room again, and there had been a corresponding change in Neil. He had stopped drinking; when he came home at nights now he had about him the scent of fresh air and the countryside where, presumably, he had been walking with Etta. He looked happier, more at ease with himself.

She should have been pleased about that, but thinking about his obsession with money which must, one day, force him to give up Etta, she was afraid for him.

An invitation to take tea with the MacKenzies duly arrived. Rowena donned her best white muslin dress sprigged with blue and her gypsy straw hat tied with a blue and cream striped ribbon and, to her own surprise, greatly enjoyed her visit to their fine house, which was similar to the Bains', but not nearly as fine as Maxwell's.

On the way home she called in at the house in Common Loan, where Ewan, as usual, had very little to say to her, and his wife stared with open disapproval at her uncovered throat and arms throughout the visit, and made cryptic Biblical references to fallen women.

As always, she sighed with relief when she found herself back on the footpath outside, her duty dispensed with for another week. She crossed Causewayside Street, then hesitated at the entrance to Gordon's Loan.

She had scarcely seen Kerr since his mother's funeral; she herself had been busy with her new duties, while he had been involved in settling Alison's business affairs and closing down the shop. She had wanted so much to see him, but the strength of her own feelings, the deep love she had discovered within her own heart on the day of the funeral, had in some way frightened her. It seemed wise to stay away, to let him be the one to decide when they should meet.

But now, when he might be only a few steps away, the longing to be with him was too strong to be denied. She began to walk along Gordon's Loan.

The shop door opened beneath her tentative fingers, and she stepped inside.

The place still smelled of sugar and cinnamon and aniseed, though the shelves were empty. The scales at one end of the counter gleamed dull silver in the subdued light from the little window. There was a strangely expectant atmosphere about the small room, as though it was holding its breath, waiting for the door in the rear wall to open; waiting for Alison Fraser to bustle in and set everything in motion again.

It was impossible to believe that she would never again take her place behind the counter. Rowena felt tears prickling her eyelids as she lifted one of the round weights from the scales. The scoop that had been used to hold the sweets clattered down as it was released. The noise was still echoing through the room when the door to the house opened and she looked up to see Kerr standing there.

'I — I was just taking a look at the shop.' She put the little weight back hurriedly as though caught in the act of stealing.

'Rowena—' He gazed at her as though he had been searching for her for a long time, and had almost given up hope of success. He stood aside, and she went past him into the kitchen, half afraid to see the room now that it was bereft of the woman who had given it its soul.

But the kitchen looked much the same as ever. The range was gleaming, the cushioned chairs waited invitingly on either side of it, the kettle crouched on the fire like a contented cat purring steam into the air.

'Philip and me know a bit about fending for ourselves,' Kerr said, seeing her glance about the place. 'We've got good neighbours too, and Ibby comes in now and then to give the place a going over.'

'I should have come to see you before this.' Guilt washed over her.

'It's me who should have called on you,' he said awkwardly, and a brief, strained silence fell between them.

'Have you decided against moving to Barclay Street?'

'No, I'm going ahead with that. I feel that mebbe my mother would have liked it. But we don't take possession of the new house for a week or two.'

Then, as her eyes fell on the big kitchen table, strewn with scribbled papers, he added, 'I was just attending to some work.'

She picked up a sheet and saw that it was covered with detailed plans. For a moment she was puzzled; then, slowly, the drawings began to make sense to her. 'Isn't this a spinning jeanie?'

He took it from her, glanced at it, looked up at her with a faint smile that told her that her quick recognition had pleased him.

'Aye. I'm trying to adapt some of them to do the work we require more efficiently. You see—' He launched into an explanation, then laughed and checked himself. 'Don't let me get started on that or I'll never stop talking.'

'I didn't know you knew how to adapt machines.'

'Most managers have to know a bit about that if they're to be of any use. I used to work with the machinery before I went on the road. Manufacturers have to try ways of improving production, you see. And when machinery's getting old and nobody's willing to spend money on getting it properly repaired the need's even greater.'

Sensitive to all Kerr's moods, she noticed the steely edge creeping into his voice. 'Is it Neil you're talking about? Is he refusing to spend the money?'

Kerr picked up the plans, looked at them, tossed them down again. 'It's nothing for you to worry about. Sit down for a minute.'

She did so, watching him as he gathered his notes in a neat pile. He was simply dressed in cream-coloured trousers and a linen shirt, open at the neck to reveal the strong smooth pillar of his throat. He still showed signs of his loss; his mouth turned downward in repose, his eyes were unsmiling.

'How's Philip?'

'Well enough. I should have come to the house sooner than this to express my gratitude to you. It was a brave thing you did that day, looking for us.' He sat down opposite her, got up almost at once and walked about the room.

'Things are quieter in the town, and yet — Kerr, d'you think there's going to be more trouble?' Remembering the noise, the frightening passion of the crowd, her mouth went dry.

'Oh yes,' he said immediately. 'The meeting agreed to work with other districts throughout the country in an effort to force reform on London, if need be. And I've no doubt that force is what it must come to.'

She recalled the mob sweeping down Storrie Street the day she and Ibby had been trapped in the doorway. 'How can ordinary working folk suddenly change so much that they try to take the law into their own hands?'

'They've not changed. They've just become desperate and worried and — frightened beyond all enduring. Paisley's always been a town with a heart to it, but now it's as if there's a storm coming that could rend that heart in two and set us all against each other. It's Philip's part in it that worries me. He's too hot-headed, too bitter to be of use to anyone. He'll only endanger himself and others if he gets caught up in such things.'

After the tirade he was silent, seeming to withdraw into his own thoughts. It was growing dark in the room, and getting more difficult to make out his features clearly. She experienced once again that great wave of love she had first known in the graveyard. It was unbearably sweet, but Rowena felt that Kerr had grown away from her in the weeks since his mother's death. She was certain that if she gave in to her impulse, if she went to him and put her arms about him, he would withdraw even further. It would surely mean the end of their friendship, and she couldn't bear that.

So she forced back her need for him, and rose to go.

The movement stirred him from his reverie. 'Wait—' he said, and moved to light the lamp on the table. 'I have something for you.'

She waited, hovering between the table and the door as though poised for flight, while he burrowed in the carved chest where, she knew, Alison had kept her clothes. When he straightened and turned she saw that he held a large shawl in his hands.

He came to her, draped it swiftly over her shoulders, then stepped back, his eyes appraising her. 'There.'

'Ohhh—' She stepped nearer to the lamp. The shawl was a fine example of Paisley's best weaving. It was made of the finest cashmere, light to wear and yet thick and warm; large enough to be folded in half and still cover its wearer as fully as a long jacket might.

The centre was white, with a small spade motif, as in playing cards, picked out in black. The deep borders, repeating the pine pattern that the Paisley weavers had taken from India, and since established as their own, held a treasure-chest of jewelled colours that almost flashed in the lamp-light.

Rich crimson and emerald green and sapphire blue sparkled back at her, skilfully interwoven in a pattern created and worked by men who were undisputed masters at their craft.

'Ohhhh—!' Rowena said again, in a soft, awed sigh. Her fingers trailed through the luxuriant red and white fringe that finished off the shawl, moved to the beautiful border, sank into the soft folds. She looked up to see Kerr watching her, smiling.

'I'm glad it pleases you.'

'It does, but—' She felt colour come to her face. 'I couldn't accept it! It's too much!'

His hands moved to cover hers as she began to take the shawl off. 'I meant it to be a gift for my mother. I was waiting for the right time, but I waited too long. She'd like you to wear it in her stead, I'm sure.'

He drew the shawl about her again, settling it over her shoulders, drawing the soft folds around her throat.

The single lamp's glow made a cave of the room, its outer fringes in shadow and Rowena and Kerr safe within a pool of golden light that softened the hard planes of his face and emphasized the green flecks in his eyes, giving them an emerald glow.

'I've pictured you in this shawl,' he said quietly. 'You look just as I thought you would. You look—'

His hands, still smoothing the soft silky material, stopped on her shoulders. His fingers tightened and held, drawing her closer.

She went willingly, her face lifted to his as he bent his head, seeking and finding her mouth with his.

She had dreamed of a moment like this, in those years while she was growing up, lonely in the midst of the bustling Bain household. Of recent weeks she had dared to include Kerr in that dream. But her imagination had not taught her that a man's arms could be so tender, the pressure of his lips against hers such a pleasurable sensation.

Kerr held her so close to him that she felt his heart thumping an irregular beat against her own body. His face was cool and smooth against hers; their mingled breath was an incense that sent her head whirling with exultation. When they finally released each other they did so slowly, reluctantly, and Kerr's hands stayed firm on her shoulders. She drew a deep, shaky breath, and was suddenly too shy to look up into his eyes.

'I've waited too long for that, too.' His voice was breathless, and his soft laugh held a tremor. 'Times it's a curse, being a Scot, for we're altogether too cautious for our own good.'

He bent to kiss her again, his mouth moving tantalisingly from her closed eyelids to her cheekbones, from the tip of her nose until, at last, it found her waiting lips once more. The tremor in his voice had spread throughout his body; she felt him shiver against her before they drew apart.

'It's getting dark,' he said huskily. 'Time you went home. I'll walk with you.'

He released her to pick up his jacket, and she was alone, more alone than she had ever been before.

The night sky, on this summer's evening, was pearl grey, tinged with sweeping brush-strokes of soft rose and palest gold above the roofs to the west. Carriages trundled past, some with lamps twinkling through the gathering darkness.

There were fewer pedestrians about than by day so they were able to progress without having to step into the roadway to avoid crowds.

They walked side by side without touching, or even speaking to each other. The shawl lay snugly about Rowena; now and then she stroked its beautiful border.

A couple came towards them, giggling together, the young man's arm close about the girl's waist. They turned in at a doorway just ahead. Rowena wished that she and Kerr could one day know a warm, comforting closeness like that.

She gave him a swift, sidelong glance, but he was staring ahead, and it was too dark to make out his expression.

Suddenly fearful, she wondered if he was regretting the mad impulse that had made him kiss her; regretting, even, that he had given her the shawl instead of saving it for someone more experienced, more mature, more worthy of his attentions.

He stopped at the Bains' gate. 'I'd best leave you here.' Then he took her hand in his. 'You're very quiet. Are you angry with me, Rowena?'

'Oh no!' Relief gave her voice more emphasis than it should have had, but she didn't care. 'I only thought — I feared that you—'

'That I what?'

She floundered for words, finally said lamely, 'Wanted the shawl back.'

'Wanted the—' he began incredulously, then suddenly took a fit of coughing. When it was over, she saw to her relief that he was smiling, his teeth gleaming white in the dusk.

'I don't want to take anything back.' He reached for her other hand and she gave it to him gladly. 'Rowena, I've a deal of matters to see on my mother's behalf. But after that, I'm hopeful that our family's debts will be settled at last. Then I'll be free to think of my own life. I've not got the right to ask you now if you'll be my wife—'

The sweetest words she had ever heard set her heart singing, and she almost missed the rest of his speech.

'—But I'll talk to you just as soon as I'm free to do so — and to Mister Bain as well.' He paused, then added with wry amusement, 'And Ewan Lindsay, come to that. Would you be agreeable to my plans?'

The first star of the evening hung in the sky just beyond his head. It glittered at her like a great diamond.

'I would,' she said, and it felt like a marriage pledge before a minister. He drew her into the shadows made by the trees overhanging the wall and kissed her again.

'My mother would be well pleased if she knew about us,' he said.

She stood by the gate, watching until he rounded a corner and disappeared, then she went along the short driveway and let herself into the house, walking slowly because at this early stage her new-found happiness lay within her heart like something made of the most beautiful, the most fragile glass.

Step by step, moving very carefully, she carried it with her up the great staircase to her room, where Ibby was putting out her night-robe and turning down the bed.

XV

Rowena's fragile happiness settled into reality as the summer weeks sped by. The shop in Gordons Loan, and the two-roomed house behind it, were sold, and Kerr and Philip moved into four handsome rooms in Barclay Street.

Since men weren't expected to know anything about domestic details, Rowena and Ibby spent their spare time at the new house, making it habitable. Kerr was content to let them see to the furnishings, and Rowena plunged happily into the task.

She said nothing to Neil of the new turn her life had taken and he, busy at the counting-house now that Fergus was away, didn't seem to notice that his sister had changed in any way. There was no sense in telling him anything until Fergus was back and Kerr had a chance to speak to him, she decided. In reality, she was nervous of Neil's reaction to her news, and was hoping that Fergus, who liked Kerr well enough, would be her ally.

He had planned to spend only a short time in Helensburgh, but his health was poor and Sarah insisted on keeping him with her. Rowena saw to it that his library was swept and dusted daily, and waited for him with growing impatience.

When, as Neil had forecast, she was surprised by a visitor while immersed in housework, it was almost inevitable that that visitor should be Maxwell King.

He arrived one fresh September morning when she and Ibby were busy beating the carpets from the drawing room. They had just struggled indoors with a fine large Persian rug which they were settling into place before the fireplace.

Rowena, head wrapped in a scarf to protect her hair from the dust, the sleeves of her serviceable brown working dress pushed back to free her slender arms, a large apron tied about her waist, was on her knees tugging at one end of the carpet when she suddenly realised that Ibby, at the other end, had stopped work and was staring at the doorway behind her.

'Stop day-dreaming and—' Her voice died away as she turned to see what the girl was gawping at, and saw Maxwell standing in the doorway, elegant in oyster-coloured trousers tucked into tall black boots, a deep blue coat and ruffled white shirt, hat in hand.

'Forgive me—' he came forward as she scrambled to her feet. 'The front door was open and I followed the sound of your voice.'

He laid his hat down on a small table, bent and caught one side of the rug, straightening it with a deft twist of his strong hands.

'There! Is that as you want it?'

'Y — yes. Thank you,' she stumbled over the words, then her wits came back to her. 'Sit down, Mister King. Ibby, fetch the Madeira — you'll have a glass, sir?'

He stayed on his feet. 'Thank you, but no. One good thing has come from these pestilent meetings on the moors — I've followed their resolve to abstain from tea, coffee and spirits, and I find that my constitution has the benefit.'

His eyes followed each movement disconcertingly as she lifted her arms to unwrap the scarf from about her hair.

'Though it's clear enough that most of the rabble who took the vow that day broke it almost at once. I can't vouch for the sales of tea and coffee, but I know there's been no danger of the local howffs closing down through lack of custom.'

She signalled to Ibby to go away, and ran her fingers through her hair, glad that she had followed the custom of having it cut fairly short. She knew, without having to look in the gilt-framed mirror, that it lay well enough in auburn curls about her neat skull.

Maxwell lifted a large book from the table by the window. A frown tucked his brows together as he studied it.

'Surely this is one of the account ledgers from the counting house?'

'Yes.' As he began to speak again she added quickly, 'I found it in Neil's room and left it in here to remind myself to take it to him. He often works late into the night at home.'

'Indeed?' He opened the book, ran his gaze down the neat lists of figures that she had finished working on only half an hour earlier. One fingernail tapped the page slowly, thoughtfully, and she caught her lower lip between her teeth as she watched.

She enjoyed working with figures and making accounts balance; Neil, on the other hand, had little patience with money when it came to book-work. His interest lay in coins that he could put into his pockets. Since Fergus had left the counting-house in his charge, her brother had taken to bringing work home so that Rowena could deftly restore order to the chaos he had created.

But it was essential that nobody should find out about it, for Neil's sake. Maxwell King was Fergus's closest friend. He had once been his partner in the mill. One word from him, even a hint that he doubted Neil's ability, could ruin her brother's future. And the fault would be entirely hers, for leaving the ledger about where it could be seen by anyone who walked into the drawing room.

Finally, to her great relief, Maxwell laid the book down without further comment. Rowena, free to move again, took off her apron, drew her sleeves down, and seated herself. Maxwell immediately took a chair opposite her, so that she had little choice but to look directly at him.

He was, she thought, a handsome man still, with his long face dominated by deep brown eyes and his dark hair greying becomingly over the temples.

'I apologise again for arriving at such an early hour, but I returned late last night from England, and I was eager to call.'

'It was kind of you, but Mister Bain's not here. He still isn't well enough to travel from Helensburgh.'

'I'd heard that. It wasn't Fergus that I came to see,' he said. 'Are you in the habit of doing the housework yourself?'

His brows rose, then descended to meet between his dark eyes, when she explained, with as much serenity as she could summon under the circumstances, that she was earning her keep as housekeeper.

'But my dear child, this is monstrous! You mean that after raising you as their own daughter Fergus and Sarah expect you to become a servant?'

'You're mistaken, sir.' Her voice was just as sharp as his. 'It was my own wish that I should find some form of work. Mister Bain gave me the opportunity to do so under his roof.'

'But you have no need to work!'

'Which makes me more fortunate than most of the other women in this town. However, I do have a wish to work.'

'By God, Rowena,' he said, 'you're the first woman I ever met who wanted to go her own way!'

'Then you must have led a most sheltered and tedious life, sir.'

The laughter surprised out of him was rich and infectious. 'I hadn't thought so until now, but you may be right.'

Then he sobered, his dark eyes studying her intently feature by feature.

'Since you're the mistress of the house—' one hand went up swiftly to stop the words trembling on her lips '—or the keeper of the house, if that's the way you prefer to think of yourself — then I shall ask you what I should more properly have asked of Fergus or Sarah—'

She folded her hands primly in her lap. 'Perhaps you should wait until they come home before you put your request, sir.'

'My name is Maxwell,' he insisted gently. 'And I'm not of a mind to await their return. My time is not only valuable where banking is concerned, Rowena; I've also reached the stage in my life where there is perhaps more sand in the base of the hour-glass than above. Whereas you have still so much of it left—'

His voice halted briefly, his intent gaze never leaving her face. Then he asked, 'Does your practical mind consider it possible that a young woman and an older man might find contentment together?'

As she grasped his meaning her heart lurched in startled shock, steadied, lurched again.

'I — I can't say, without knowing the people concerned.'

'Ah, but you do know them.' He rose, began to pace back and forth across the rug he had just helped to lay.

'I'll be honest with you — for I feel that nothing less than honesty will do where you're concerned, my dear Rowena. My first marriage was made in my youth, as romantic a union as a man could ever wish. I think I told you when you visited my house that I've been a childless widower these past fifteen years. I've my health still, and I've been most successful in my business. But of late—'

He stopped pacing. For where she sat, head bent, she could see his shoes, planted firmly on the rug. She knew that he was looking down at her, but she couldn't bring herself to lift her head in case her eyes told him that her heart was already promised.

'Of late – since knowing you, Rowena—' he went on, after a short silence, 'I've been aware of a desire to recapture something of the youthful passion I once knew, before the sands run out altogether. I fancy I could do so, with your assistance.'

There was another brief pause. She could think of nothing to say, other than a silent prayer that somebody, anybody, would come into the room and put an end to this impossible proposal of marriage.

'On the practical side,' Maxwell King proceeded, 'I've many financial interests, most of them paying handsome dividends. I need – I want a son to inherit my money. I intend to retain my home here, though I must spend a great part of my time in England from now on.'

Now he was speaking more as a businessman, his voice crisply confident as he listed his assets. 'My wife would find herself mistress of more than one comfortable residence. She would travel with me and meet people; I can assure you, Rowena, she would have every reason to be content with her lot.'

His feet had moved away. The colours of the Persian rug merged together under her panic-stricken gaze. The silence was longer this time, and she knew that he was waiting for her to speak. She raised her head, and quailed as she saw unexpected gentleness and, worse still, hope in the dark eyes that surveyed her.

'Mister Ki—'

'Maxwell.'

'Max – Maxwell.' She stumbled over the name. 'I – you've taken me by surprise, sir, and I—'

'If you truly had no knowledge of my growing interest and admiration, then you must also be the most modest woman I know.'

'I have to remind you that I'm not the Bains' daughter. I'm not a gentlewoman—'

He brushed the argument aside with an impatient wave of one hand. 'For that matter, I'm not high-born myself. I judge people by what they do with their lives, not by their beginnings. And you're a lady, Rowena. I knew when I saw you acting hostess in my own drawing-room that you'd make a fine wife for a man such as myself.'

As he talked, Maxwell walked back to the window, picked up the ledger once more, weighed it in his two hands. 'I'll allow that I've said too much all at once. You shall have time to get used to the idea – but in the meantime I hope that I'll be permitted to call on you?'

She couldn't even give him that amount of hope. She took a deep breath and began to say, 'I must – I feel that I—'

The front door opened and closed and footsteps tapped crisply over the tiled entrance hall. Maxwell's face stiffened with resentment, while relief made Rowena feel quite faint. Then Neil was in the doorway. His eyes went at once to the visitor, then to the book in Maxwell's hands. His jaw dropped, and a look of pure consternation spread over his face.

Rowena sprang to her feet, talking swiftly before either of the men had time to speak. 'Oh, Neil – you've come back for the ledger. I saw that you'd left it in your room, and fetched it down here for you—' She went to Maxwell King, took the book from him, and held it out to Neil.

'I've just been telling Mister – Maxwe—' Confusion almost tied her tongue in a knot, 'Mister King—' she said at last, not daring to look at Maxwell, '—that you often bring work home to do at night.'

There was relief in her brother's blue eyes as he took the ledger from her.

Maxwell King left shortly afterwards. Together, brother and sister accompanied their visitor to the door and watched him unhitch his horse's reins from the wrought-iron frame that had been installed there for that purpose.

He swung himself easily into the saddle, nodded to them both, and turned his mount towards the gate. He rode well, sitting straight-backed and confident in the saddle. Now that she was freed from the need to reply to his proposal, Rowena found that the realisation that such a man could even consider that she was fit to become his wife was briefly flattering.

'Thank goodness I managed to prevent you from saying anything about the ledger when you came in,' she said happily to Neil, a feeling of euphoria sweeping over her now that her unexpected ordeal had ended.

But as far as her brother was concerned the business of the ledger was over and done with. His face was flushed with humiliation, and gratitude was far from his thoughts.

'You look like a servant,' he said crushingly. 'For goodness sake go indoors and wash your face. God knows what the man must think of us!'

And he strode off down the drive without another word, the ledger tucked securely beneath his arm.

She glanced into the hall mirror and saw to her horror that throughout Maxwell King's entire visit, proposal and all, she had had a dusty smudge right along one cheekbone and over the bridge of her small neat nose.

XVI

The house in Barclay Street was almost finished to Rowena's liking. She and Ibby had enjoyed putting it to rights, limited through they were by the amount that Kerr could afford for furnishings.

He had allowed himself to use some of the money realised by the sale of his mother's house and shop in Common Loan. By the end of the year he hoped to pay off his father's debts fully. After that, he explained to Rowena, he must do what he could to help Philip. Then, and only then, would he be free to consider his own future.

She reached up on tip-toe, drew his face down to hers, and

kissed the place where his brows were drawn together between his eyes.

'We've got plenty of time, you and me,' she assured him. 'If Philip was better placed he could have a home of his own, then he could marry Ibby. And I couldn't come to live in Barclay Street while he's there.'

A frown puckered her own forehead now. 'I wish I knew why Philip dislikes me so much.'

They were walking on the braes above the town on a blustery October day. Smoke from the chimneys below streamed off to one side instead of gathering as it often did in calmer weather. She could make out the ruins of the great Abbey, and the High Church spire, and the ribbon that was the River Cart, flanked by the old town on one bank and the new town, built in the former Abbey grounds within the past fifty years, on the other. Another ribbon of water, narrower and with fewer twists and turns in it, marked the canal.

'He's disliked everyone ever since Waterloo, except perhaps Ibby and myself,' Kerr was saying when she gave him her full attention again. 'You live at Carriagehill, and he mistrusts people with money—'

'I've no money! If I had I'd pay your debts and make you marry me at once.'

'But you live in one of the finest houses in the town. In his eyes, you're Fergus Bain's daughter. And Neil does little to help matters.' His voice hardened and he quickened his step without realising it. 'He behaves in the mill as though he had a God-given right to be an employer instead of an employee. He's an arrogant fool, without thought for anyone but himself!'

Her happiness in his company was dimmed. 'Your brother dislikes me, and my brother dislikes you even more.'

'Philip, as I've said, has little liking for anyone. As to Neil's reasons — I can think of nothing I've done to cause such ill-concealed hatred.'

He was walking over the springy turf so fast that she had to run for a few steps now and again to keep up with him. The wind caught at the back of her large shawl and made it billow like a ship under sail.

'It makes my work at the mill almost impossible at times,'

Kerr was saying when she caught up with him again. 'We see little of each other, thank the Lord, but with one of us responsible for the money going out and coming in, and the other responsible for the day-to-day work of the machines and the thread production, we must make mutual decisions now and again. Each time, it's as though he's more bent on thwarting me than doing what's best for the manufactory. D'you think he's found out that I intend to marry you?'

The very words brought a glow to her heart. 'I'm certain he hasn't. Neil's too interested in gambling and card-playing — and courting Moira MacKenzie — to give more than a passing thought to me.'

The wind, frustrated by the firm grip she had on her shawl, was busy trying to wrap her skirts about her legs, making it almost impossible for her to keep up with Kerr's long steps. She was forced to ask plaintively 'Could we not walk more slowly?'

He stopped, surprised, then laughed as he realised how breathless and harried she was. 'You should have said so before. Here—'

He put his arm about her and led her down a slope to a sheltered spot where she could sit on a rocky outcrop that thrust its way through the grassy surface, and get her breath back. She was glad of the respite, for there was something that had been worrying at the back of her mind, and she had decided that she must tell him.

'Kerr, Maxwell King called on me a few weeks back.'

'Oh—?' he said absently, his eyes on her face, examining each feature with possessive pride. 'And what did Mister King want?'

Then his brows suddenly shot up and his jaw dropped with sheer surprise as he read her expression. 'What?' he exploded. 'You and—? But he's an old man!'

'He's not old! Well, not terribly old. Anyway, he's what you might call well-preserved.'

'And what you might call wealthy.' Kerr turned away, strode to where a rowan tree flaunted its treasure of crimson berries against the cloud-strewn sky. 'I suppose any woman might feel that all that money would compensate for all those years.'

'You're being offensive!'

'You refused him, of course.'

His back was to her, but his tone was as chilly as the wind, the final two words more of a command than a question.

A prickle of anger edged her voice. 'No, I didn't.'

Kerr's hand closed on the rowan's slender trunk with murderous intent. 'So you accepted his proposal.'

'He didn't propose − not exactly. Neil came in and interrupted him.'

'But you gave him to understand—'

'He asked if he might call on me. Because of Neil, I wasn't able to give him an answer.'

His hand was white-knuckled on the tree-trunk. 'How fortunate for you. It means that you still have two suitors. Two of us begging for your hand.'

'Kerr!' She bounced from the rock and pummelled at his back in her exasperation. When he merely twitched his shoulders as though she was a fly that could be thrown off she marched round him until she could look up into his face. It was closed to her, eyes hooded and mouth tight.

'Kerr, how could I refuse him permission to call on me without letting him know that I care for someone else? If he knew that he'd mebbe talk to Neil about it, then Neil would want to know. It's best to wait till Mister Bain comes home. He's got a high regard for you − he'll help us.'

His eyes, when he finally looked at her, held pain and vulnerable uncertainty. 'Perhaps,' he said, 'you'd be wise to consider marrying with Maxwell King. He has so much to offer you. I've got nothing but hope for a future that might be years away yet.'

'I'd as soon wait and hope with you.'

His grip relaxed a little on the tree. 'You might be quite old yourself by that time.'

She put her arms about him. 'Never as old as you, though.'

At last, to her relief, the stiffness went out of his body. He laughed, and freed the poor rowan tree so that he could hold her. Then they ran, hand in hand, over the windy moor.

*

One of the shops in Causewayside Street had a very nice dark blue brocade that might do nicely for the parlour curtains in Barclay Street. Rowena hesitated over the material, almost bought it twice, and finally decided that Kerr, much as he hated being involved in such matters, must make his own decision.

With a small cutting of the cloth in her pocket, she walked to the mill to see him.

Since that first visit when Fergus acted as guide she had been in the mill on several occasions. The thump and rattle of the water machinery no longer made her uneasy, but she still felt, when she climbed the rickety stairs, that she was inside a living, breathing being, a being with little or no regard for the puny humans who laboured within its entrails.

She knew better, now, than to open the door of the scutching room; she climbed past it, and past the carding room where the cotton was drawn into thick strands of roving ready for the spinning jeanies. Now and again she met men and women and children, some of whom nodded and smiled in recognition. Most of them, especially the children, crushed themselves against the fragile banisters to let her pass, eyes shyly averted, drawing away from her so that the cotton fibres clinging to their clothes didn't contaminate her warm dark green pelisse.

Their deference both embarrassed and humiliated her, but as she neared the floor that housed the first of the spinning rooms she was almost sent tumbling back down to the landing below as a boy came running out, eyes bright and mouth agape with excited importance, and rushed past her without seeming to realise that there was anyone else on the stairs at all.

Breathless, confused, and not a little frightened, she clung for a moment to the shaky railing, listening to the sound of the lad's precarious flight, expecting at any moment to hear the thump of flesh and bone on implacable timber as he lost his footing and rolled down a whole flight of stairs. But he seemingly reached the ground floor unscathed, for the outer door flew open then slammed shut and she was left to complete her climb to the landing.

Nobody noticed her as she went into the first big room. The jeanies were still busy spinning the roving into thread, their spools whirling tirelessly, but as they worked their wheels most of the operators near the doorway were craning their necks to see what was going on in a nearby corner. Rowena followed their eyes and saw a few men and women gathered about Kerr, who knelt beside a machine that had come to a standstill.

A small body — pitifully small, she realised as she saw it measured against Kerr's big capable hands, was being carefully eased out from beneath the jeanie. At first she thought that the child had been injured by the machine, then he was clear of the frame and she saw that his thin little face was flushed with fever, his body racked with uncontrollable shivering.

'Give me room, damn it!' Kerr said fiercely to the people crowding closer to look at the boy. He tore his jacket off and wrapped it about the child, who was bare-footed and wore only a thin shirt and patched, tattered trousers. As he gathered the small body into his arms and got to his feet Rowena saw that his face was frightening in its anger.

He walked to the door without seeing her. She was certain that she felt a wave of searing heat from the child's fevered skin as he went by. She followed him onto the landing in time to see Neil, stylishly elegant in pearl grey trousers with a russet coat and sky-blue cravat, hurrying up the stairs, the boy who had almost knocked her down close behind him.

'What's amiss?'

'This.' Kerr held out the child in his arms.

'A child? You send for me to come across from the counting house just to see a sick child?'

'A mere babe who was set to work in the spinning rooms — on your instructions, I'm told, and without my knowledge.' Kerr said with savage contempt. 'He'd nowhere to go when he wasn't at work, so he was sleeping beneath the machines. Nobody to watch out for him, so he'd to beg what food he could get from the other workers — not that they could spare much. I found him under one of the machines, ill and like to die from hunger and the stench of the oil in his lungs. And it's your doing, Neil Lindsay — deny it if you can!'

Neil's blue gaze tore itself free of the other man's, moving to Rowena and the men and women who crowded at the spinning room door, listening avidly. His pale skin flushed a deep scarlet.

'The boy needed work. I took him on in good faith!'

'There was none of this trickery,' said Kerr, 'when Mister Bain had control of the place.'

He stepped forward, and it was Neil's turn to snatch at the rail as he was almost dislodged from the top step by Kerr's broad shoulder. As she followed him down Rowena heard her brother snarl at the open-mouthed audience 'Get back to your work or get out of my mill!'

She was hard put to it to keep up with Kerr as he stormed out into the yard. A cart had just been unloaded and her father and a few other men, including Philip Fraser, were hauling the bales of cotton across the cobbles to the store.

'Kerr—' She plucked at his shirt sleeve, and he swung round and put the child into her arms.

'Hold him.' He caught her about the waist, lifted her, together with her burden, effortlessly, and deposited them both in the cart. Then he swung himself onto the bench beside the driver.

'I've work for you to do – you'll be back in a moment,' he added crisply as the man opened his mouth to protest. 'Or would you as soon step down and let me drive your horse myself?'

Meekly, the man gathered up the reins and clicked his tongue. As the cart bumped across the bridge Rowena looked back and saw the group of men from the stores watching in stunned disbelief.

At Barclay Street they put the child, muttering and quite unaware of what was happening to him, to bed.

'A nervous, debilitating fever which can be brought about by a number of causes,' the physician announced after making a swift examination.

'Including neglect and lack of proper food and shelter,' Kerr commented, and the man nodded.

'Quite so. Where's his family?'

'The women in the mill tell me he was raised by his grandmother. She abandoned him after finding work for him a few days ago.'

'So he's a pauper,' the physician said briskly. 'Employed at Watson and Bain's, you said? And only six or seven years old by my estimation.'

'About that,' Kerr agreed, his eyes on the child.

'D'you not know, sir, that under the Act recently put through

Parliament by Peel it's against the law to employ children under nine years of age in a textile manufactory?'

Now Kerr lifted his head. Rowena almost flinched away from the look in his eyes. 'I know that, but it seems that the man who took him on is quite unaware of it.'

'Aye — well, it's early days yet, and no doubt many an employer's unwittingly breaking the law. It would be wrong to condemn them harshly for it.' The medical man's voice was indulgent. 'As to the child — you'll require me to see to it that he's taken to the Poors' Hospital—'

'So that they can finish the job that Neil Lindsay started?'

The man flushed. 'I happen to be one of the physicians in attendance at the Hospital and I can assure you, sir, that the care the paupers receive is of the highest standard!'

'He stays here until he's recovered sufficiently for me to find someone who'll take him in. I asked you here to treat him, not to preach to me as to his place in life!'

There was a short silence then the other man said huffily, 'A little brandy to stimulate and restore his senses. Perhaps some bleeding or purging—'

'Or some broth to fill his belly, and plenty of warmth and care,' Rowena broke in, and this time Kerr's eyes rested on her with quick appreciation.

'It seems to me that these would be of more value than leeches and blistering,' he said, and the physician, clearly deeply offended, took his fee and departed.

Together they worked over the child, spooning a little brandy between his lips, stripping his filthy clothes off, sponging the thin little body with warm water then dressing it in a shirt of Kerr's. Then Rowena made gruel and they managed to feed some of it to their patient.

'How will you manage to look after him?' she asked when they had done all they could and the child had fallen into a fretful, tossing sleep. Kerr followed her into the kitchen and dropped into a chair, stretching his long legs across the rag rug that she remembered so well from Gordon's Loan.

'Mistress Forbes might agree to come in every day and see to him until he's better. Then I'll find someone willing to take him into their family.'

Suddenly he looked bone-weary, yet there was tension in every muscle; an angular stiffness over-sat the way he sprawled in the chair.

'D'you know the child, that you're so willing to do all this for him?'

'Nobody knows this child. Nobody even knows his name. But he deserves better than he got at the mill.'

Love for this prickly man who could so unexpectedly reveal different facets of his nature, welled up in her. She went to him, stroking back the familiar errant strand of hair that lay across his forehead.

His hand moved swiftly to trap her fingers and hold them against his lips. His eyes, as he looked up at her, were brilliant, the green flecks accentuated.

'It must be a terrible thing, Rowena,' said Kerr against her palm, 'to have nobody in the world to call your own.'

*

Before going back to Carriagehill Rowena called in to see Mistress Forbes, the neighbour who saw to the housework for Kerr and Philip two or three times a week. The woman, bright-eyed with curiosity at the new turn of events, agreed to help to nurse the child.

Neil came in for his evening meal in a towering rage.

'How dare Kerr Fraser brawl with me in front of the mill-workers!' He poured a generous measure of Fergus Bain's brandy into a glass and threw himself onto the sofa.

'Is it true that you took that boy on to work with the spinning jeanies?'

'Must you always take his side against mine?'

'Kerr says the boy's only about seven years of age, Neil.'

He shrugged. 'I assumed he was small for his age. We need someone of his size to make a proper job of cleaning under the jeanies.'

'But Kerr says—'

He finished the brandy and got to his feet. 'I've no wish to know what he says! He's a trouble-maker, and the old man was a fool to bring him back into the mill!'

She followed him into the hall, watched as he began to climb the stairs.

'Neil, why d'you hate him so much? Have you forgotten that he saved your life, and mine?'

He stopped half-way up the curving staircase, his hand suddenly white-knuckled on the rail.

'Yes, he saved us, but he didn't save her, did he?' said Neil. 'Neither of them did. They saved us — but they let her drown!'

She watched him continue up the staircase. Although the house was warm, she shivered.

XVII

As Rowena's confidence in her own ability to run the house competently in its mistress's absence grew she began to entertain on a modest scale, inviting girls she had met at her dancing classes.

Often, as she dispensed tea in the drawing room, she wished that Alison Fraser could have been there.

She missed the older woman sorely, whereas she was guiltily aware of a light-hearted sense of freedom as far as Sarah's absence was concerned.

Neil looked upon the social gatherings with approval, but even so, she couldn't bring herself to tell him that she had plans to ask Etta Brodie to call at the house.

Etta's invitation had been in her mind for some time; she had visited the girl on several occasions during her illness and had grown to like her very much. The young school-mistress's affection for Neil was obvious, although she tried hard to conceal it.

Rowena had intended to call in at the mill school-room to see Etta, but before she had time to do that she met the girl in a shop.

Etta's pale face flushed scarlet when the invitation was issued. 'Oh, Mistress Lindsay — I couldn't do that!'

'My name is Rowena—' She was reminded, briefly, of Maxwell urging the use of his Christian name on her not so long ago '—and I don't see why you couldn't.'

'Mistress Bain wouldn't approve.'

'Mistress Bain's in Helensburgh, and so's Mister Bain. And their housekeeper, for that matter. For the moment,' said Rowena blithely, 'I'm the mistress of the house, and free to invite my own friends. I've been given hospitality in your home,' she added, her stomach tightening at the very memory of those cups of strong tea she had choked down, '—and now I want to return some of that hospitality. Besides, I've some clothes and some books that might be of use to the schoolroom children and I want you to come and have a look at them.'

Even when it was decided, she didn't tell Neil that Etta was coming. He would be at the mill, and it was up to Etta to choose whether or not she wanted him to know that she was to visit his home.

On the appointed day, at precisely the appointed hour, Etta scurried up the gravelled driveway like a frightened mouse, and gazed about her with startled wonder as Rowena opened the front door and she stepped into the hall.

'It's — it's beautiful!' She let Rowena take her shawl, her large dark eyes studying the wide sweep of the staircase, the fine ceiling high above, the dark panelled doors.

She wore a dark red dress trimmed with cream lace, and her hair was well-brushed and neat. The dress was old, and neatly darned in places, but spotlessly clean.

Rowena led the way to her room, where the books and clothes she had promised Etta lay on her bed. When they had been inspected, she took her guest on a tour of the house. The girl's eyes, already huge in her pale thin face, were like saucers as she looked about her.

A fire had been lit in the drawing-room grate, for autumn was well and truly with them and the day was chill. Etta accepted a cup of tea gratefully, but scarcely ate anything.

During her tour round the house she had begun to relax a little. Now, toasting her feet at the fire, sipping her tea, she was finally at her ease, talking about the schoolroom, the children, her hopes and plans for them.

Watching her over the rim of her cup, Rowena saw that the other girl's face had become thinner since her illness. Indeed, it was almost gaunt, the flesh phased out to reveal the fine bone-structure that, together with those brilliant, vivacious eyes, made Etta a beauty. Her hands, as she accepted another cup of tea, were so fragile that it seemed that they might shatter if one held them tightly; her dress, though neatly cut, seemed a trifle loose, as though the body within it had very little substance.

'Does your brother know that I'm here?' Etta asked in a sudden straightforward way that caught Rowena by surprise.

'No. I felt it best to leave it to you to tell him, if you wished.'

The flush that always sat on Etta's high cheekbones deepened slightly, though her eyes didn't waver.

'I suppose you know that we meet, from time to time.'

'Yes, I know. I can tell when Neil's been with you. He's always—' she sought for the right words, and Etta waited calmly, '—always happier when he's been with you. More at ease within himself.'

'I'm glad of that. Some folk seem to find Neil difficult to understand, but not me. To tell you the truth,' said Etta simply, 'I love him.'

'And he—?'

'I'm quite certain that he loves me. He's brought me more happiness and contentment than I ever knew in my whole life before.' She glanced down at her tea-cup; fragile and delicate though it was, the egg-shell china looked clumsy against her long thin fingers, with their scrupulously clean nails. Then she looked up at Rowena again as she went on, calmly, 'But he shall probably marry with Moira MacKenzie.'

The words almost took Rowena's breath away. 'But why, when you've just told me—'

Etta smiled. Her earlier shyness and hesitancy had gone; in their place was a maturity and strength that Rowena had never seen before.

'D'you not see, Rowena, that your brother needs more from life than I can ever hope to give him – even if I was well? Neil has to have—' She started to cough, but managed to control it, then sipped at her tea before going on. 'He must always be safe.

He has to feel that he's protected, and wealth is the best form of protection there is.'

'Etta, that's nonsense!'

'For you, mebbe. Even for me — but not for Neil. Think what would happen to him if he married me — not that he ever would, and not that I'd let him if he wanted to. He'd have a sickly wife to support, and little chance of children. He'd have to live in a cottage, or a few rooms somewhere, and he'd have to worry about money from dawn till dusk. No—' she shook her head decisively. 'I'd not want that for him. Not for Neil. Moira MacKenzie's a nice lassie, from a good family. She thinks well of him — doesn't she?' she added with a trace of anxiety that cleared when Rowena nodded.

'I'm glad. She'll look after him.'

'And you?'

Etta laid her cup down and folded her hands in her lap.

'Oh, I shall make certain to keep myself out of his life once he decides to ask Moira to be his wife. So you see, Rowena—' a sparkling smile lit her face for a moment, '—if you invited me here with some idea of black-footing, there's no sense in it, for Neil and me were never meant to be husband and wife, and no amount of plotting will change things.'

Then the colour flared, rose-like, in her face as the door opened and Neil walked into the room.

He halted in the doorway as he took in the sight of the two of them seated by the fire, the tea-table between them. Then he came forward, his eyes fixed on the thin girl in the dark red gown who rose with natural grace to meet him.

'Etta?'

'Good afternoon, Neil,' she said, with more composure than either of the Lindsays. Rowena, startled by her brother's sudden, unexpected appearance, was motionless; Neil, after a quick unguarded happiness in his eyes when they first fell on Etta, was clearly finding it hard to know how best to react.

'Your sister kindly asked me to come and collect some books she has for the schoolroom — and some clothing that I can use for the children.'

She had given him her hand when he came into the room. Now, since he showed no sign of relinquishing it, but stood motionless, his eyes still fixed on her face, she drew it carefully from his grasp. 'And now, Rowena, if you'll excuse me I must go.'

'I'll fetch the books—' Rowena escaped upstairs, leaving the two of them alone for a few minutes. When she came back they were in the hall, Neil carefully tucking Etta's thin shawl about her shoulders as though she was Royalty and the shawl an ermine-trimmed velvet cloak.

'I'll carry these.' He took the bundle from Rowena's hands, carefully avoiding looking directly at her. Unexpectedly, Etta kissed her; again, as she put her hands on Etta's shoulders, Rowena had the feeling that there was no substance to the girl, that she was already a spirit from another world. But the lips that brushed her cheek were warm, the smile Etta gave her as Neil opened the door was filled with affection.

'Thank you for a lovely afternoon,' she said, and then the door closed, and Rowena was alone.

She went quickly into the drawing-room and watched from the window as they went down the drive. Etta's hand rested lightly on Neil's arm and all his attention was on her as she talked, her free hand gesticulating for emphasis.

Rowena hoped that her decision to ask the young school-mistress to the house wouldn't cause trouble between the two of them, but as they reached the gate and disappeared from her sight she saw her brother laughing, and knew that, for these two at any rate, everything was all right.

As to her own fate, when Neil returned for his evening meal, she had no idea. But she had the right to choose her own guests, she told herself firmly, and began to clear away the tea-things.

*

The meal was a quiet affair. After it, as he pushed his chair back and got to his feet, Neil said abruptly, 'Since you seem so fond of entertaining these days, no doubt you'd be agreeable to holding a small dinner party?'

She gaped at him, startled and apprehensive. 'A dinner party? But I've never tried to do that before.'

'You've organised them on Aunt Sarah's behalf, and the servants know well enough what's expected of them,' he said impatiently. 'Next Friday, I thought. It doesn't need to be anything too grand.'

'How many people should we invite?' The first shock had passed, and already her mind was racing ahead, planning a menu.

'Moira and her parents. And perhaps Maxwell King, to make up the numbers. He has a fondness for you, and he always enjoys an opportunity to visit this house.'

As he went to the door she said to his back, 'We could invite Kerr too.'

His shoulders stiffened, and his voice was coolly dismissive when he said, 'Mister and Mistress MacKenzie, Moira and myself, you and Maxwell King. The numbers would be wrong if we invited another man.'

'Then invite another woman.'

Neil's eyes were almost navy-blue with anger when he turned and looked down on her. 'If you're about to suggest Etta Brodie, don't trouble yourself. I'll not have it!'

'Because she's only the schoolmistress, or because you don't want to sit at the same table as both Moira and Etta?'

'Mind your own business, Rowena,' he said, his voice low. 'Moira and her parents, Maxwell King, and the two of us. Nobody else.'

*

The dinner party was a great success. Despite all Rowena's misgivings and her increasing nervousness as the evening approached, nothing went wrong. Afterwards, in the drawing-room, she carefully saw to it that she and Maxwell were never alone, in case he pressed her for an answer to his proposal.

As the party was so small, her aim was achieved easily enough, although she was aware of his eyes on her almost throughout the entire evening, and was certain that the others must have noticed it too.

Neil was relaxed and at his most charming, attentive to Moira and her mother, giving Maxwell and Mister MacKenzie the polite deference due to them as older men, and successful men into the bargain.

'By God, Fergus and Sarah made a wise choice when they

elected to raise the two of you,' Moira's father said when the guests were leaving. 'You're both a credit to them, and I shall tell them so when we next meet!'

Moira and her mother kissed Rowena before they left, and Maxwell brushed his lips over her fingers.

Carriage wheels crunched over gravel, and the Lindsays were alone, their first dinner-party over. Neil's eyes sparkled, and he gave his sister a most unexpected hug.

'Every inch a lady,' he said jubilantly. 'The MacKenzies were impressed – and so was Maxwell.'

Whistling, he went off to bed, well pleased with himself.

*

He was still in a good mood the next morning when he left for the mill. Rowena, well pleased with herself, walked down to Causewayside Street to buy some ribbons she needed for a gown she was making over for the winter. All she needed to do to make it look like new, she thought as she stepped out briskly, was to lower the neckline a little, remove the rather fussy lace edging from the sleeves, and add bunches of ribbon to the skirt.

She went into a shop that she often patronised, and was greeted by the woman behind the counter, who willingly brought out box after box of ribbon so that Rowena could make her choice. Then the shop-keeper measured and cut and parcelled the purchase.

'I was sorry to hear about the mill schoolmistress,' she said chattily as she handed the little parcel over and accepted payment. 'She was in here often – always such a pleasant wee soul.'

'Etta Brodie? What's happened?'

But she knew, by the look on the woman's face, the expression of gloom tempered by a certain mournful pleasure at being the first to bring the news, what had happened, before she heard the words.

'She died in the night. At least it was a quick ending. Her poor mother was always that frightened that Etta would end up in the House of Recovery, the same as her other bairns. But no, it happened at home, before they could think of taking her away. Goodness only knows what'll happen to the old folk now, for it was Etta's earnings that kept that family going—'

But Rowena was already blundering out of the shop, running along the footpath, bumping into people and swerving, when necessary, out into the roadway if a group seemed likely to stop her.

She was breathless when she reached the counting-house. The senior clerk looked surprised and somewhat disapproving when she burst in.

'Your brother? He's gone home. He seemed a little unwell—'

She was back out in the yard again, her legs protesting at the demands she was making on them. It was going to be a long, uphill run to Carriagehill. For the first time in her life, she wished that she had adopted Sarah's custom of travelling everywhere by carriage.

A cart that had just been unloaded was rumbling across the bridge. The traffic on the main road was busy, and the driver reined in his horse. Then he looked down, surprised, as Rowena tugged unceremoniously at his trouser-leg.

'Are you going by Carriagehill?'

He put a hand to his cap, recognising her. ''Morning, mistress. Aye, I'm to go up over the back to collect my next load—'

'Will you take me to the Bains' house? I must get there quickly!'

For a moment the man looked confused and embarrassed, then he shrugged. 'It's not near as comfortable as a carriage, but—'

'Please!'

'If you're certain it's what you want—' He reached a calloused hand down to her and hauled her up to sit on the seat beside him. The horse moved forward and Rowena clung grimly to what handholds she could find as they lurched and jolted onto Causewayside Street.

She saw, but didn't heed, the startled faces upturned to her as she went by on the cart. She was in a state of shock, unable to take in the fact that Etta was dead, aware of nothing but the need to go to Neil.

He was in the drawing-room, standing by the window, looking out at the shrubbery. She recognised the pose – it was Neil's way of shutting other people out. He didn't turn when she came into the room.

'I've just heard the news about—' She couldn't say the name. Instead she went to him and put a hand on his arm. He let it lie there.

'We shall have to find a new schoolmistress,' he said in a cold, tight voice.

'I'm sorry, Neil. I know that you were—' she stopped, started again. 'I know that Etta loved you.' His arm jerked, as though the muscles had gone into a spasm. 'She told me so when she was here.'

He turned slowly and stiffly, moving like an old man. His face was grey to the lips; even his eyes had lost their colour.

'She was – the only person I knew who demanded nothing of me,' he said, speaking in an awkward way, as though his mouth couldn't move properly. Then he added, 'Leave me be, Rowena.'

She stepped back, her hand falling helplessly to her side, and watched as he walked out of the room.

Slowly, step by step, he mounted the stairs. He didn't reappear until the following day. She never heard him mention Etta Brodie again.

Ten days later, in early November, a week before the anniversary of his mother's death, Neil Lindsay became formally betrothed to Moira MacKenzie.

XVIII

Sarah and Fergus Bain made the journey from Helensburgh to celebrate Neil's betrothal to the only child of a wealthy Paisley manufacturer.

Rowena was shocked to see how much Fergus had aged. He had to be helped into the drawing-room, where he sank into a chair with a sigh of relief.

Sarah's doll-like prettiness was still apparent, but she had acquired a small double chin and her rings were beginning to sink into her podgy fingers. Her sharp eyes took in the drawing-room at a glance as she settled herself in the deep sofa before the fireplace.

'You seem to be managing very well, Rowena.'

Margaret, the girl Rowena was trying to train as a parlour maid, brought in tea. The tip of her tongue was visible between her teeth as, cross-eyed from watching the tray she carried, she inched her way across the carpet. Depositing her burden, un-spilled, with a gusty sigh of relief, she began to scurry out before remembering what she had been told. She backed up, dipped an untidy curtsey in Sarah's direction, and fled to the safety of the kitchen.

Sarah had a flood of complaints about Paisley. The streets were dirty, the houses flanking them seemed so dingy, the chimney smoke caught at her lungs.

'And there were men loitering at every street corner and look-ing at me with open insolence as I drove by.'

'I'd not have called it insolence,' Fergus said mildly.

Rowena poured more tea for her foster-mother. 'It's true that there are silk weavers unemployed just now — over a thousand looms lying idle because the silk gauze trade's failed.'

'Satan finds work for idle hands,' Sarah said ominously,

sounding so like Ewan Lindsay's wife that Rowena almost giggled.

'Who's going to find food for their empty bellies?' she countered instead, and Sarah gave her a long, cold look.

'I see you've still not learned to control your tongue, Rowena. I'll have an oatcake, if you please. I hear there was another meeting at Meikleriggs Moor recently.'

'Yes, but the folk who attended it were well-behaved.' Including, she thought with relief, Philip Fraser.

'Maxwell told us, when he visited Helensburgh—' Sarah paused to sip her tea, and Rowena, who had not known of Maxwell's visit, stared down at her hands, reluctant to meet the older woman's eyes, wondering if Maxwell had spoken about his interest in her.

But it seemed not, for Sarah's voice flowed on, '—That the people flaunted flags through the town, for all that they'd been banned. And there were arrests — or are you going to tell us that Maxwell made the whole story up?'

'No. There were arrests, as he said.'

'That doesn't sound well-behaved to me.'

'I said the folk who attended the meeting behaved themselves. It was another matter where the militia were concerned. They rushed in and arrested eight musicians from Neilston — men who'd done nothing more criminal than play a piece of music that's been banned.'

Then, to her great relief, Neil came in, and she was forgotten in the warmth of Sarah's welcome.

There was no question of Fergus taking over the mill again. Twice a day a man came to wheel him out in an invalid chair; with great difficulty he managed to get into the counting house on a few occasions, but he couldn't attempt the mill with its narrow, worn shaky stairs.

Kerr called several times to see him on business, and there was no shortage of friends to keep his evenings happily occupied. In Helensburgh, Fergus had discovered the pleasures of card games and chess. As long as he had partners he was contented enough.

He and Rowena talked a lot during the day, when Sarah was out shopping or calling on old friends.

'It's strange how painlessly the mill reins slipped through my fingers once I got used to the idea that I could no longer control them,' Fergus told her. 'You'll find as you get older that life's like a series of rooms. You think you want to stay in one for ever, then something happens to force you out, the door closes behind you, and soon the new room's just as good as the old one – and so it goes.'

He gave her a swift, shrewd glance. 'But mebbe you've already found that out for yourself. I suppose you still visit your father?'

'Yes. He's – getting older.'

'We all are, lass. Neil's done well for himself. It'll be your turn soon, no doubt. Are you still as independent as ever? It'll disappoint Maxwell if you are.'

She had been intent on the mending in her lap, but dismay brought her head up swiftly. 'He spoke to you?'

'He's a very proper man, Maxwell King. Naturally he'd want my blessing and my permission to court you.'

'You gave it?'

'I told him it was your own concern, but I'd not stand in his way. I said nothing to Sarah,' he added as she stared at him in consternation. 'If I had she'd have been in Paisley within the day, getting the banns cried. He's a good man, Maxwell. Old enough to be your father, I know that, but still, he'd be a sound, solid husband. But that's your own business. We must all make our own way in life.'

Then he added, enigmatically, 'And when you look at me with those bonny brown eyes you got from your mother, lassie, I'm moved to wish that I'd dared to take a different turning when I was younger, and be damned to the consequences.'

*

The gathering that Sarah Bain held to mark Neil's betrothal was to be the most important social event of 1819. The house was scoured from attics to cellar and its inhabitants, including the servants, all got new clothes for the occasion.

Sarah even hired liveried footmen from Glasgow, to Fergus's spluttered annoyance.

'We're not the Court in London, woman!'

'You'd deny me the pleasure of seeing that everything's done right?' Sarah demanded, the light of battle in her eye. This was the moment she had been waiting for since the day she first took on her ready-made family, and she was determined to have a gathering that Paisley would never forget.

'I'll have you know, Fergus Bain, that Mistress MacKenzie's bringing a new and very dear friend with her. A widowed lady from Edinburgh who's staying in Paisley at the moment — and I'll not have her going back to Edinburgh and telling the gentry there that we don't know how to entertain in Paisley!'

'I doubt if Edinburgh'd be interested,' Fergus growled, then, having the wit to recognise a superior opponent when he saw one, he said no more.

Sarah went her own way, as they had both known she would, and the liveried footmen were on duty in the hall when the guests began to arrive, hurrying into the lighted house from their carriages, urged up the steps by a keen northerly wind.

The drawing-room was a glittering jewel box of colour. Fergus held court from his favourite chair by the fire, while his wife, a stately galleon in cream silk, moved among her guests.

Mistress MacKenzie and Moira, normally a somewhat plain girl, but tonight so flushed and bright-eyed with excitement that she looked glowingly pretty, arrived late and overflowing with apologies.

'When we went to fetch Elizabeth we found that her little girl's not well — they've taken rooms in Garthland Place, you know — and Elizabeth insisted on staying with her until she went to sleep. My husband sent us on in our own carriage, and he'll escort her here as soon as possible.'

Mistress MacKenzie took her place in the welcoming committee, with Sarah on one side of her and Neil, at his most handsome in a coat that was the same vivid blue as his eyes, on the other, Moira on his arm. Flustered as she was by the betrothal of her only child to such a charming man, and further flustered by her own tardy arrival, Moira's mother chattered like a sparrow as the guests flooded into the house.

'How pretty you look, Rowena — we shall have another wedding on our hands directly, shan't we, Sarah? — Jane, my dear, so good of you to come — Elizabeth worries so about that child, you see — Oh, Mister King, you flatter me! — Being a widow I suppose she feels even more responsible for the child — Lexie, I've never seen you look so handsome, my dear — A very rich widow, of course. Her husband was a glove manufacturer who made a fortune. Her house is quite beautiful — Wilhelmina, how good it is to see you—'

Rowena would have loitered in the hallway, watching for Kerr's arrival, but Maxwell drew her into the parlour by his side.

'I regret that I've been too pre-occupied with business in Lancashire to call on you.' His eyes drifted over her simple green muslin dress, trimmed at the low neckline, the waist and the sleeves with white lace, in a way that told of his approval.

'And we've been pre-occupied with preparations for this—' she indicated the crowded room, 'so I should not have been very good company anyway.'

A smile touched the corners of his mouth. 'Allow me to be the judge of that.'

Neither Kerr nor Mistress MacKenzie's Edinburgh friend had arrived by the time the reception line broke up and came into the parlour to join Rowena and Maxwell. Sarah and Moira's mother were busy trying to top each other's grand plans for the wedding when one of the footmen announced the long-awaited arrival.

With a short scream of pleasure Mistress MacKenzie plunged into the throng and made her way to the woman who had hesitated in the doorway. Not, Rowena realised at once, because she was unsure of herself, but because she was taking time to scan the people in the room before allowing herself to mingle with them.

She heard, quite clearly, Neil's indrawn breath as he looked up and saw the newcomer. A moment later the Edinburgh glove-manufacturer's widow was with them, drawn into their midst by her triumphant hostess.

Mistress Melville had long-lashed eyes of a remarkable violet colour. They were set in an oval, smooth-skinned face framed by midnight-black hair which hung to her exposed shoulders in fashionable ringlets.

Her clothes, too, were in the very latest style — so much so that the fashion had not yet reached Paisley, which lagged sorely behind Edinburgh and Glasgow in that respect.

Mistress Melville's slender figure was dressed in a silk gown the colour of fine sherry; it was low-waisted compared to the other dresses in the room, with a full skirt, puffed sleeves, and a low neckline that left her white throat and shoulders bare, apart from a necklace and earrings of glowing rubies, and allowed a glimpse of the upper slopes of her fine breasts.

The dress was trimmed with silver gauze, as was the elaborate turban on her head, another innovation in Paisley. The turban was also wreathed in silver ribbons and finished off with a cluster of small soft white feathers.

She greeted them all with composure, quite undismayed at being the only stranger among people who had known each other for years. Something — a long-buried memory — niggled at Rowena. She felt that she had seen this woman before somewhere.

Her voice was a strangely attractive blend of the Edinburgh lilt and something flatter and broader, tending towards the West of Scotland.

'Tell me, Mister King, do you still own the linen thread manufactory in Barrhead?'

Maxwell's eyebrows rose. 'Until a year or two ago. Then I sold it.'

'At a fine profit, I trust?'

'Well enough.' He eyed her narrowly. 'Is it business that's brought you to Paisley?'

She smiled. 'In a way.'

'But how did you know about my manufactory?' he asked, and her smile widened.

'I know quite a lot about this part of the world, Mister King. Tell me, with all your business interests, have you ever considered going into Parliament?'

'I've dabbled with the notion.'

'A man of your abilities should never dabble, sir, he should plunge both hands into life and seize every opportunity he can think of. I myself would have enjoyed politics had I been a man. It is most unfair,' said Elizabeth Melville 'that women are not able to enter Parliament.'

'You see yourself as a champion of the downtrodden?' There was mockery in Maxwell's voice. He studied the newcomer with a calculating, faintly suspicious gaze, quite unlike the open admiration that Neil, oblivious to the fact that his betrothed was by his side, was displaying.

'On the contrary,' Mistress Melville said crisply. 'I subscribe fully to the view that we shape our own destinies. The strong hold the power, and the weak must go to the wall. That's as it should be in a properly ordered world.'

Thinking of the little boy Kerr had carried from the mill, Rowena felt a shiver run down her spine. She moved away, happy to leave Elizabeth Melville to the others.

Kerr was very late. Rowena, who had scarcely seen him since Sarah's arrival tied her to the house, was pacing the hall impatiently by the time the footman opened the front door and he stepped inside, eyes flaring with surprise and a touch of amusement at the sight of the livery.

Then he saw Rowena, and the hidden mirth spread into a warm smile.

The second footman helped him off with his coat and carried it off. Kerr adjusted the white lace at his wrists and brushed an imaginary speck of dust from the sleeve of his dark green coat; more lace foamed at his throat, accentuating the firm lines of his face.

As she went forward to let him take her hands in his he said, low-voiced, 'You look very beautiful tonight.'

She smiled up at him. 'I'm so happy to see you! I wanted to come to Barclay Street, but Mistress Bain found a hundred reasons to keep me here. The child — is he well?'

'He's fine.' There was a pleased lilt in his voice. 'He's up and about, no thanks to that physician and his leeches and his purges. They'd have killed the bairn for sure. There's a woman in the carding room willing to take him—'

'For payment that you'll have to find.'

He shrugged, pausing in the drawing-room doorway. 'You can't expect working folk to feed an extra mouth without help. They're fine people, Rowena. They'll be good to the boy, and they don't expect much from me in return.'

'It's still more than you can afford. It's Neil who should be paying the child's keep, not—'

She stopped, suddenly aware that she had lost his attention. He had gone quite white, his eyes fixed on the other side of the room.

'Who's that?'

She turned to look, and tried to fight down a prickle of jealousy. 'A new friend of Mistress MacKenzie's. A rich widow from Edinburgh.'

'Introduce me,' Kerr said, and moved purposefully towards the group by the fireplace, looking neither to right nor left.

By the time she caught up with him, Mistress MacKenzie herself was fussing over the introductions, and Kerr was holding the tips of Eizabeth's white-gloved fingers while Neil looked on in smouldering silence.

'Mister Fraser—?' The violet eyes surveyed him with amused interest.

'Your servant, Mistress Melville—' Kerr raised her hand to his lips, then added, as he lowered it again, 'And — welcome back to Paisley, Eliza.'

It was only then, as they all stared at him in surprise and the widow from Edinburgh said calmly, 'I felt sure that you, at least, wouldn't have forgotten me, Kerr,' that Rowena realised where she had seen the woman before.

Years ago, at Waingaitend, watching the stage-coach take Kerr away from Paisley, turning to find out who he had been searching for, seeing the vivacious dark gypsy-like girl. The girl who had left Paisley shortly after he did, and had now returned.

Kerr's former sweetheart, the girl his mother had expected him to wed, had come back into his life.

XIX

Sarah Bain couldn't quite make up her mind whether Mistress MacKenzie had lost a social point in befriending a woman who had grown up in a two-roomed cottage in Espedair Street, or gained a point by virtue of the fact that Elizabeth Melville — Eliza Wilson that was — had clearly torn free of her humble roots and done very well for herself.

'It seems to me,' Fergus said at last, when he could bear no more of her chatter about it, 'that a self-made woman should be judged on the same standing as a self-made man. Accept the woman for what she is, and be content with knowing that her presence helped to make your betrothal party a success.'

'But why should she come back?' Sarah wondered aloud, and Fergus groaned and made his way slowly and painfully, with the use of two sticks, to his library, where he could be certain of some peace.

Rowena, too, wished that she knew the answer to that question. Elizabeth Melville had smilingly refrained from answering it. She had said very little about herself, concentrating instead on looking and listening, as though anxious to soak herself in Paisley's atmosphere again.

Rowena recalled Alison Fraser telling her that none of Elizabeth's family were left in the town, so the woman hadn't returned to seek out her kinfolk. She couldn't stop remembering, as though it had been recently, the look on Kerr's face as the stage-coach carried him away that day, or how his eyes had fixed on the girl's lovely face until the coach turned and hid them from each other.

The woman had quite dominated the gathering, she thought as she fetched a basket and went out to the shops, ignoring Sarah's instruction that a servant should be sent in her stead.

Poor Moira, the bride-to-be, had been quite eclipsed.

Maxwell King had been intrigued by the newcomer, Neil openly dazzled, and as for Kerr — he had watched and listened to Elizabeth Melville as though mesmerised.

If this was jealousy, Rowena didn't like it, because it hurt. She deliberately forced it from her mind, concentrating on the shopping list she had written, scurrying from shop to shop to escape the chill wind that had persisted for the past few days, ever since the night of the party.

Unable to stay away from Kerr, she bought some sweets for John, the little boy he had rescued from the mill, and went along to Barclay Street. It was noon, and Kerr would probably be at home.

But it was Mistress Forbes who opened the door and stood aside to let her in. 'Kerr's not in from the mill yet, but no doubt he'll be along to see the lad.'

She laughed indulgently, leading the way into the warm kitchen. 'You'd think the child was his own flesh and blood, the way he frets about him. Mind you, it makes a pleasant change to see a man so gentle and caring.'

John, still stick-thin, all eyes and tumbling fair hair, thanked her shyly for the sweets then almost snatched the paper-wrapped package from her fingers. Rowena was reminded of the day she had first met Alison Fraser, and taken sweets back to Neil as a peace offering.

'The wee soul's been that used to starving,' Mistress Forbes mouthed at Rowena over his head, then she removed the bag from John's hands with a rapidity that more than matched his own and put it up on the high mantelshelf out of his reach.

'You can have these when you've eaten your dinner, and not before, my laddie. Och, would you look at my good clean washing, blown down across the kail bed! John, come and help me. Your legs are better at running after it than mine are.'

As the two of them hurried out of the back door to rescue the runaway washing, the door from the street opened and shut. Rowena, about to go and help Mistress Forbes, stopped and turned back into the kitchen.

'Kerr—'

But it was Philip Fraser who came in, his hazel eyes instantly hostile when he saw her standing in the middle of the room.

'Kerr's at the mill.'

'Is he not coming home?'

'I don't know.' Philip took his coat off, threw it over the back of a chair, and lifted the lid from a pot on the range.

Then he replaced the lid and turned to face her, his jaw jutting forward aggressively. 'You might as well get back to your fine house and your fine brother.'

'I'll wait.'

'You'll not,' said Philip flatly. He picked up her basket, held it out to her. And there was something about the way he stood there, motionless and yet menacing, that stopped the angry words in her throat. She took the basket from him, and went out of the house.

A smart carriage drew up as she reached the end of the road. Elizabeth Melville's lovely face appeared at the window.

'Rowena! Are you walking all the way to Carriagehill, my dear? I'll take you there.'

'Thank you, but I can walk—'

'Charles—' Elizabeth said, and the coachman, already down on the footpath, politely but firmly removed the basket from Rowena's hand, opened the carriage door and handed her in, putting the basket on the floor by her feet.

Elizabeth, dressed today in deep blue velvet trimmed with a rich black fur, sat back and beamed at her guest.

'How pretty you look. The strong wind's given you a most becoming colour.'

Fully aware that it was suppressed rage with Philip rather than the wind, Rowena coloured even more. 'Is your daughter recovered from her illness?'

'A little better. She has a weak chest, poor lamb, and she's seldom well enough to go out of doors in the winter. The physicians say that she may improve as she grows older.'

'I wonder that you brought her to Paisley at this time of year. You surely recall that this town has more than its share of chest complaints.'

'I remember everything about Paisley,' Elizabeth said sweetly. 'But Anne and I have been inseparable since her birth, so I couldn't think of leaving her behind in Edinburgh.'

'Your business here must be urgent.'

'No,' said Elizabeth Melville thoughtfully. 'Not urgent. But I believe in acting as the mood takes me. After all those years I' suddenly felt that I must return to Paisley for a short while to — renew old friendships.'

'Such as your friendship with Kerr?'

'You're quite head over her heels in love with him, aren't you?' said Elizabeth.

'Why should you think that?'

The older women's mouth curved, though there was no laughter in the deep violet pools of her eyes.

'Very well — keep your secrets and your illusions. But perhaps not all your illusions. You must grow up sooner or later.'

She tossed a folded scrap of paper onto Rowena's lap. Pride prevented Rowena from opening it.

'I like you, Rowena — may I call you Rowena? You're not a fool. You're young — you still have time to learn from someone who has lived longer and seen more of the world.' Elizabeth leaned forward, her eyes brilliant. 'Use men, Rowena, but never let them use you. If power's a sword, a clever woman can duel just as skilfully as any man. I look forward to teaching that to my own daughter as she matures.'

When they reached Carriagehill she declined Rowena's invitation to go on.

'Anne will be waiting for me. And I've promised to go horse-riding this afternoon.'

Standing on the steps at Carriagehill, watching the carriage move smoothly out of the gate, Rowena realised that the piece of paper Elizabeth had tossed into her lap was still crumpled in her hand. She smoothed it out.

In the strong square fist she had first seen on papers scattered across the kitchen table in Gordon's Loan the night he kissed her for the first time, Kerr had written across the page 'Eliza — I must see you.'

*

'Has she invited you to her lodgings in Garthland Place?' Kerr asked.

'No. We're not well acquainted, and besides, I understand that her daughter doesn't keep well.'

She had decided before she saw him again that she wouldn't mention the note Elizabeth Melville had so casually, and so maliciously, given her. She had made up her mind that she wouldn't mention the woman at all. But to her fury, Elizabeth's name had scarcely been off Kerr's tongue in the ten minutes since they'd met.

Rowena snuggled her hands deeper into her muff and looked down at the grey canal water. They were walking along the towpath, a pleasant enough place in summer, when wild poppies and foxgloves and delicate pink wild roses admired their reflections in the water. Now, the vegetation on the banks was dead, the canal's surface mirroring a grey sky above.

'What age might the child be? D'you know?'

'About the same age as John, I believe.'

Ibby had told her that last September some Paisley men, Philip among them, had gone to collect twenty-four pike handles that had been made for them in Johnstone, the little town at the end of the canal. The weapons themselves had already been made secretly in Paisley.

But the militia were watching the roads and stopping anyone they suspected of being involved in the general unrest that still seethed through the country, Ibby said.

So Philip and his friends had tied the pike handles into a bundle and floated them down the canal, walking innocently along the towpath just as she and Kerr were walking now, until they were safely hidden in one of the tunnels, the one nearest the west end of the town. Then they had lifted the handles from the water and smuggled them into a nearby loom shop.

'About six or seven years old—' Kerr's voice was as bleak as the weather.

Ibby said that there was a growing stock of weapons in the loom shops. Somehow, the men had even managed to get some pistols. Ibby said that the weavers at Maxwellton, on the west side of the town, knew how to make bullets. Ibby was mortally afraid of what Philip might do if any of these weapons fell into his hands.

'What did she call the girl?'

She stopped thinking about revolution and dredged in her memory for the name.

'Anne, I believe.'

'Anne.' He said it as though tasting the name on his tongue. 'Rowena, I want you to invite Eliza to call at Carriagehill with the child.'

'Her little girl's not able to go out just now. It's too cold.'

'Then you must go to Garthland Place and call on her.'

She stopped walking. 'I don't like her, Kerr, so why should I visit her?'

His face was alight with purpose. 'To see the child. To see if the child resembles Eliza or — or someone else.'

A chill that had nothing to do with the weather, or with the threat of revolution, gripped her. 'Someone else? You?'

He stopped walking. His hands came up to hold her elbows. 'Rowena, we were sweethearts — Eliza and me — before I went away from Paisley. That was some eight years ago. If this child's seven years old then she could be mine. She could be my daughter. I must know. I must know!' he insisted as she said nothing, but stood within his grip, staring up at him.

'You think that might be why she's come back to Paisley? To face you with your own child?'

His hands fell away from her. He turned and began to walk on. 'It's not that. I've tried to meet with her, but she evades me every time. If she's come back on my account it can only be to taunt me. To let me know that I have a daughter, then to refuse to permit me to see her.'

'But what if Anne should be your daughter, Kerr? What could you do then? She's the very centre of her mother's life. Elizabeth wouldn't give her up to you. Or—' the chill deep within her was worse, freezing her heart until she thought it would have to stop beating altogether '—or have you some thought of offering her marriage, for Anne's sake?'

'I don't know,' Kerr said, and there was torment in his voice. 'I don't know what I'd do if I found out that the girl was mine. I only know that I must see her. I must know the truth! And you must help me, Rowena—'

But she had turned and started back along the path, walking fast, dragging her skirt impatiently from a strand of bramble bush that tried to catch at it. He didn't follow her, and she didn't look back.

She rounded a corner, and was out of Kerr's sight. For a moment she allowed herself to stop, and put up her hands to cover her face.

Never, never, never would she visit Elizabeth Melville. For one thing, she had no wish to meet the woman again. For another—

For another — she couldn't bear the thought of seeing Kerr's eyes, Kerr's tawny hair, Kerr's wide mobile mouth imprinted on another woman's child.

She started walking again, hands clenched into fists inside her muff, and got back to Carriagehill shortly before Neil came in, windswept and remarkably cheerful.

'How's poor Moira's chill?' Sarah asked, and he had the grace to look guilty.

'I've still to call on her. I was horse-riding over the hills near Barrhead.'

'What an uncomfortable pastime.'

'I like it,' Neil said defensively.

'You hated it when you were a child. I'd no idea that you'd taken it up again,' Sarah, more interested in her embroidery than in the conversation, spoke absently.

It was then that Rowena remembered that Elizabeth Melville also liked horse-riding.

XX

A long, cruel winter had already announced its arrival, but the colder weather did little to ease growing tension.

Paisley was garrisoned by men of the 10th Hussars and the 13th Infantry, together with a regiment of yeomanry and a volunteer rifle corps hurriedly recruited by the Earl of Glasgow and Paisley to safeguard the rich from the poor.

'Who—' said Rowena wryly when Ibby brought the news, '—will protect the poor from the rich?'

The militia shivered and grumbled in their spartan quarters. To add to their miseries, they were sometimes stoned by children when they were seen out in the streets, particularly in the west end of the town, where feelings ran high.

As Parliament continued to dither the unions slowly gained strength. It was common knowledge now that bullets were among the weapons being made in some of the weaving shops. House doors were pocked with little holes where the apprentices practised their skills with cleggs, spiked iron darts.

Clandestine meetings held under cover of the dark nights were attended by strangers speaking English dialects difficult to follow. Rowena heard that a large Staffordshire plate had been broken into pieces, and some of those pieces given to the Scottish union leaders. When the call came and the leaders on both sides of the Border united, the shards would stand as identification.

At that final meeting the Staffordshire plate would be put together to become whole again, symbolising the workers' solidarity.

In December Ewan Lindsay and his wife both fell sick of the influenza that stalked the town.

It was Ibby who brought the news to Rowena after she paid a visit to her home.

'My mother'd see to them, but the fever's already in our house—'

'She's got more than enough to do, and they're not her kin.' Rowena's quick mind was already juggling with a list of items she must take with her to Common Loan. 'It's my place to nurse them, nobody else's.'

She realised as soon as she saw them that her father and step-mother were both very ill. The woman sitting by their bed looked up with visible relief on her thin face.

'Thank the Lord you're here, lassie. I've two of my own wee ones sick, and my man coming in for his dinner any minute now. Most of us round here are busy nursing our own folk—'

'So will I,' Rowena hung her shawl on the nail at the back of the door, took her bonnet off, rolled up her sleeves and set to work.

Even in illness Ewan Lindsay's second wife was a grim, silent creature, lying in bed with her wiry grey hair parted in a straight line along the crown of her head, then in two plaits over her shoulders. In contrast to her husband, who tossed and muttered in his fever, she was silent, her mouth either pulled into a thin line or silently shaping words which Rowena supposed were prayers, or perhaps psalms.

Night and day came to mean little to the three of them. The fire in the range had to be kept going constantly to heat water bought from the water-carts that patrolled the streets. The sick couple had to be sponged and changed, dosed and soothed, and persuaded whenever possible to take some nourishment.

Ewan became so difficult to manage in his delirium that Rowena dragged through the truckle bed she had once slept on in the little back room, and managed after a long struggle to transfer his sweating, burning, thrashing body from the wall-bed. That way it was easier for her to tend to both patients, though it meant that there was scarcely a free patch of floor in the kitchen and she was forever hitting her shins painfully off the iron corners of the bed.

She dozed in a chair by the fire whenever she could find a few minutes, listening for a change in her step-mother's breathing or the scuffle of blankets that indicated that Ewan, in his delirium, was trying to get out of bed to go off to work.

Over and over again, as his fever neared its crisis, father and daughter re-lived the canal boat disaster that had changed their lives. The *Countess of Eglinton* heeled over, people spilling from her deck into the water. Rowena was forced to listen to Ewan searching for his wife, and never finding her.

Then all at once, on the morning of the last day in the year, he stopped tossing and opened his eyes, fixing them firmly on her face. It had been years since her father's gaze had been so blue and youthful and confident.

'You're a good wee lassie, Rowena,' he said firmly. 'Take my hand, now—'

She laid down the damp cloth she had been using to cool his face and gave him her hand. His fingers closed over hers, and for a moment she was a little girl again, safe in her father's care.

From that moment, Ewan Lindsay began to recover.

Neil had stayed away. On the few occasions when the door-knocker rattled she answered it eagerly, thinking that it might be him, but it was always someone else — the physician, who could do little now, or a neighbour enquiring about the Lindsays, or Ibby, offering help that Rowena always refused.

'I don't want you to risk taking the sickness to Carriagehill. Mister Bain's frail enough as it is.' She blocked the doorway, refusing to let the other girl in.

'You look fair worn out. You'll make yourself ill!'

'I've no intention of falling ill — I can manage fine,' Rowena said, and heard the words ring in her own ears with a hollow note.

Her step-mother died quietly and quite suddenly, with no fuss whatsoever, early one morning. Ewan, now on his feet again, though shaky, insisted on following the coffin and paying his last respects.

'Then you'll fall sick, and I'll have to nurse you again!'

'No,' said Ewan with the convalescent's petty obstinacy. 'I've survived. My times's not come yet.'

There had been snow on the wind the night before the burial and the day itself was very cold. There was another funeral going on in a far corner of the graveyard, another little knot of people tending to their dead. Standing beside her father,

Rowena pitied the grave-diggers who had had to work at the chilled ground to make a place for the coffins.

Feet shod in good strong boots crunched along the path between the gravestones. She looked up swiftly, Neil in her mind, and saw Kerr, in warm dark coat and tall hat, a few yards away. His grey eyes met hers, a faint smile touched the corners of his mouth. As he took his place by her side his arm lightly brushed hers. It was the first time they had been together since she had left him on the tow-path. His presence now was so comforting that tears filled her eyes.

Ewan stooped and lifted a handful of frozen soil; he held it for a moment, as though passing on some of the warmth from his own living flesh; then he moved forward and let his hand open. The earth fell on the coffin with a dismal thud.

As they left the bleak graveyard the other burial was just finishing and its mourners slowly dispersing. Already Rowena could see another handcart approaching along the road, bearing another plain box attended by another group of mourners.

Kerr looked at the sky, which was low and oppressive. 'We're in for more snow. And I'd not be surprised if the river froze. I'd best see to it that we're ready to close the sluice gates in time. We'd not want the wheel to be damaged.'

'Without the water-power, can the mill go on working?'

His eyes rested on her face. 'Aye, as long as there's plenty yarn for the hand-operated jeanies to spin. Neil will have ordered extra roving from Lancashire by this time.'

Then he had to hurry back to the yard, and Rowena walked slowly back to the cottage with her father to begin the task of setting the place to rights now that there was no more sick-nursing.

Ewan sat by the fire, watching as she worked about the place and made a meal for them. When she was setting the food out on the table he rose and fumbled in the leather purse he always kept on the mantel shelf. Then he held a coin out to her.

'Lass, put your shawl on and step along the road to Peter Marshall's howff for a jug of ale. You can fetch some tobacco too.'

For a moment Rowena thought that the fever was back and he was rambling. But his eyes were clear and steady.

'But father—' she said weakly, and for the first time since her mother had died, she saw the corners of Ewan Lindsay's mouth lift slightly.

'I've buried two wives now, Rowena, and I've mourned long enough. As for Martha's beliefs—' it was the first time Rowena had heard the former Widow Bothwell's Christian name '—it seems to me that if the Lord couldn't spare even one of my women I'd as soon look to my own business from now on and leave Him to look to His. Go on, now — my throat's got a ten-year thirst!'

*

Two hours later he drained the last of the ale and set his glass down with a satisfied sigh. Then he reached for the old pipe he had produced from the depths of a cupboard, where his wife's eagle eye had somehow failed to find it, and began to fill it with tobacco.

He looked as though he was well on the way to a full recovery.

'Now you'd best be getting back home, lass.'

'Let me stay here.' It was an echo of the past. 'I can look after you—'

Ewan shook his head. 'You don't belong in a wee cottage.'

'I don't belong at Carriagehill.'

It was true. Born into the working class, raised by the upper class, she now swung helplessly between them, with no firm ground beneath her feet.

Ewan worked at the pipe with a skill he hadn't lost. 'Carriagehill has more to offer. You've got all your life before you, Rowena — you must make your own way as best you can. Don't make any changes until you're certain they'd be for the best.'

She was putting on her shawl and bonnet, and he had managed to get his pipe lit, when he said abruptly, 'You're a good daughter. I could wish Neil had half your sense.'

'You'll be proud of him yet.'

'I'm not so sure,' Ewan said. 'Kerr Fraser, now — there's a man I'd be proud to call son. I got the feeling, seeing you and Kerr together, that you care for each other.'

She said nothing, her fingers fumbling with her bonnet strings.

His blue eyes surveyed her through a haze of pipe-smoke.

'Pride's all very well, lass, but it makes a poor bed-fellow, especially when you're young and the blood's coursing through your veins.'

Her hands stilled on the bonnet strings. He was right – oh, he was right, and she wanted Kerr so much that she could scarcely bear the pain of the wanting. But wanting wasn't enough – it had to be shared, and at the moment there was no indication of that from Kerr Fraser. So she blinked back the weak tears that had suddenly come uninvited to her eyes, and finally managed to tie a neat bow beneath her chin.

As she was going out Ewan said, half to himself, 'If you ask me, he's not remembered to order that roving from Lancashire.'

'What did you say?'

He looked up, and this time his eyes were troubled. 'I'm talking of Neil. The last time I was in the store, the day the fever first came over me, there was no extra roving, and no word to make room for any either.'

He hunched himself forward in his chair, staring into the glow that could be seen through the bars of the range.

'If he lets the manufactory down, God knows what'll happen to the poor souls who'll find themselves thrown out of work.'

*

A week later the frost had settled on the town like a grey pall. It seemed to Rowena that the people moving about the streets had become spectres, mere wraiths of human beings, as grey as the sky and the ground and the air between.

Ice crackled underfoot and the earth was as hard as iron. The gardens were graveyards filled with the frozen skeletons of last year's plants and bushes.

Some of the town's wells froze; water slopping from over-laden pails carried from those wells still in operation turned to ice almost as soon as it fell to the footpaths.

Work on the new jail and Bridewell on the river bank, where the Cart flowed through the centre of the town, came to a standstill; the thick stone walls, unfinished, stabbed up at the bleak sky line like the stump of a massive rotting tooth.

Some two hundred yards further up-river the great water-wheel at Watson and Bain's mill slowed and stopped. The water-powered machinery used to prepare the cotton for the spinning jeanies came to a standstill.

Rowena had been to the dressmaker's shop on the old bridge. She had collected several parcels for Sarah, and was returning home with them in the carriage when she saw that the mill yard seethed with people at a time when the workers would normally have been at their machines. Some of them were already beginning to come across the bridge, their faces grim, one or two of the women in tears.

'Stop here, William.' Sick with foreboding, she scrambled down almost before the coachman had had time to rein the horse in.

The bridge into the yard was built at a point where the river narrowed. Looking down at it, Rowena saw that there was ice forming at the banks, where grasses obstructed the flow of water. In the centre, where it usually ran fast, the water was sluggish.

'The wheel's been stopped and there's not enough roving left for more than a few hundred of the machines,' an elderly man told her bitterly. 'And they'll not be in work for long if the wheel doesn't start up again soon. No roving brought in — and no chance of any coming up from England quickly in this weather either.'

His face, creased with laughter lines, was sombre, his eyes dark with worry. 'How am I to feed my family?' he asked, and passed on without waiting for a reply, knowing full well that she could give none.

'Mister Bain wouldn't have let us down like this,' a woman said, and tossed her head angrily when her companion, eyeing Rowena, shushed her. 'I know who she is! Isn't it enough that they're content to let us starve? Do we have to mind our manners as well?'

The others weren't as bold, but as Rowena made her way across the bridge many of the people passing her stared and muttered, and one or two deliberately jostled her.

Most of the workers had gathered in the yard, their attention centred on the old building that held the counting house. Rowena saw that Philip Fraser was in the forefront.

'Come out, Neil Lindsay!' His voice echoed in the cold grey air. 'Come out and tell us to our faces how we're going to manage without work to do!'

The clerks' faces glimmered whitely through the grimy glass panes. For a moment it looked as though the people in the yard were going to storm the counting house, then the door opened and Neil appeared on the steps, to be greeted by a chorus of jeers.

'Where's the Lancashire roving?' someone wanted to know.

'Still in Lancashire!' someone else shouted, and there was another burst of abuse.

'I didn't halt the wheel! I didn't stop the machinery and throw you out of work!' Neil bellowed at the top of his voice. 'Kerr Fraser did that! I ordered the wheel to be kept going – ask him and he'll tell you, if he's got the courage to face you!'

Kerr pushed his way through from the mill and Neil pointed an accusing finger in his direction.

'There!' he yelled to the sea of faces beneath him. 'There's the man you should be reviling and threatening! There's the man who closed the sluice gates!'

Kerr's face was tight with his anger as he bounded up the steps to stand beside Neil, facing the crowd.

'Listen to me, all of you! The river's freezing over. The gates had to be closed to drain the mill lade. If we left them open for much longer the wheel would be locked in solid ice. You know as well as I do that ice can break it, then the machines'd be halted for weeks!'

'He didn't have to halt it as early as this—' Neil almost screamed. 'It could have stayed in operation for two days more – three days more—'

Kerr rounded on him. 'There's ice forming in the water now, man! It would have been crushed by tomorrow morning!'

'What we want to know is, why's there no roving in the store, Neil Lindsay?' Philip shouted again, and Neil's cheeks suddenly flared with crimson fury.

'Damn your eyes!' he roared at Philip, at the lot of them. 'The roving'll come when I decide – not you! I'll not be dictated to by a pack of wild dogs! Get back to your machines, those with work still to do. The rest of you — get out of this yard before the militia comes to hunt you out!'

Despite his bad leg Philip Fraser moved swiftly, swarming by his brother, catching Neil by the lapels of his warm tobacco-brown coat, shaking him as a terrier would have shaken a rat.

Kerr wrenched the two men apart, almost throwing Philip to one side.

'There's going to be no—' he began to shout, then his legs were swept from beneath him as Neil, his face twisted with fury, his mouth shaping itself into that old square grimace that Rowena recognised from long ago, kicked out savagely at him.

The crowd was suddenly silent as Kerr fell. He rolled, and got swiftly to his feet again, in the yard and free of the steps. Neil, springing after him to finish him off, ran right into Kerr's fist and reeled back, his hand going in shocked disbelief to his mouth.

The mob fell back to leave a space where the two men faced each other, circling cautiously before Kerr sprang in. Neil met him half-way and they grappled, feet slipping and slithering on the icy ground.

They were fairly well matched. Neil was the slighter of the pair, but sheer rage, the crimson anger that he had had since childhood, made him a formidable opponent. He tripped Kerr up, threw himself on top of the other man, his hands closing round Kerr's throat. Kerr managed to kick him off, regained his feet, and hurled himself at Neil again.

As they moved across the yard the crowd, roaring and whooping, shaped and reshaped itself into the walls of an arena. Rowena found herself trapped, unable to get to the two men who fought fiercely on the stretch of ground between counting house and mill.

They were up again, facing each other, when she managed to gain the edge of the circle. Both faces were bloody; one sleeve had gone from Neil's jacket, the other was badly torn at the shoulder. Kerr, who had run from the stuffy mill atmosphere when the crowd first began shouting for Neil's blood, had only been wearing trousers, shirt and waistcoat. His cravat had been torn off, his waistcoat was in tatters about his broad shoulders, his shirt-sleeves ripped where he had come in contact with the ground.

'Stop it!' she screamed at them, but the words were lost in the crowd's excited baying. Not quite lost, perhaps. For a moment Kerr glanced in her direction; for a moment his guard was down, and it was then that Neil hit him, a well-placed blow that sent Kerr reeling backwards towards the small platform overlooking the mill-wheel.

If his foot hadn't caught on the edge of the platform, sending him sprawling on the wooden planks, he might have crashed through the flimsy barrier and right onto the big iron buckets set in the rim of the wheel to scoop and empty water as the wheel circled.

For a heart-stopping moment Rowena thought that she was going to see him smashed to a bloody pulp before her eyes. Then he crashed onto the planks and Neil threw himself forward, hands reaching out again for his enemy's throat. At last Rowena managed to break through the tight-packed circle of men and women and ran across the slippery yard, moving like a drunken woman as patches of ice tried to trap her and send her sprawling helplessly.

By the time she reached them the men were on their feet, grappling again, both of them pressed tightly against the creaking wooden railing that edged the platform.

She pulled with all her strength at the nearest arm, still clad in shreds of tobacco-brown. Neil swung to one side, throwing her off as he did so and trapping Kerr between his body and the railing. Both men were gasping for breath now, so intent on their struggle that neither of them realised she was there.

She staggered, regained her balance, saw the immense waterwheel, menacing in its stillness, looming just behind Kerr's tawny head. Far below him, as he fought, the half-empty mill lade waited, cold and still, the first tissue of ice beginning to touch its surface.

The railing creaked again, then gave a loud, ominous crack.

'Kerr!' The cry was wrenched from her very soul. He twisted himself away from the edge of the platform and lunged, forcing Neil back. Someone took hold of Rowena's shoulders from behind and whisked her off the wooden platform onto the yard's cobbles.

'Stop it!' Ewan Lindsay thundered, tearing the two younger men apart with a strength that belied his grey hair and holding them, one in each fist.

'Enough! D'you think this is going to answer any of our problems? Lend a hand here!' he roared over his shoulder, and men came from the crowd, slightly shame-faced now that their blood-lust had been halted, to help him.

Neil was still beside himself with anger. 'I'll see you damned, Fraser! If you ever set foot in this mill again, or in this yard, I'll have the militia on you!'

Kerr threw off the men who held him and drew the back of one hand across his face, looking with disinterest at the blood it collected.

'I'd not give you the satisfaction,' he said, and began to push his way through the crowd towards the bridge. Philip stepped forward to meet his brother, and Neil pointed a shaking finger at him.

'You can get out too—' he raved. 'You've caused trouble for the last time. You'll never work here again!'

Philip took one deliberate step towards him and spat on the ground, almost at Neil's feet.

'Look to yourself, Neil Lindsay,' he said, low-voiced but chillingly clear. 'Look to yourself − one of these fine days I'll have you between the sights of a pistol, and by God I'll—'

'Philip!' Kerr's voice cracked like a whip. With one bruised and bloodied hand he caught his brother's shoulder, whirled him about, and half-dragged him across the bridge.

Slowly, the crowd followed. Without a glance at his sister or his father Neil walked across to the counting house and went inside. Ewan glanced at his daughter, opened his mouth to speak, closed it again, and went back to his store.

Rowena found herself alone, suddenly aware that the bitterly cold wind was striking through to her very bones. Shakily, she walked across the yard and over the bridge to where William, bright-eyed with curiosity, waited for her beside the carriage.

XXI

Philip's face, when he opened the door and saw Rowena on the step, settled into a scowl.

'You're not welcome at this house!'

'I want to see Kerr.'

'Have you not done enough to us, you and your brother? I wish to God Kerr'd let the two of you drown in the canal that day—'

A hand, the knuckles puffy and discoloured, landed on his shoulder and twitched him aside. The door opened wider. 'You'd best come in,' said Kerr.

At a look from his brother Philip slouched away and left the two of them alone. Kerr led her into the kitchen.

'How's Neil?'

'He'll live.'

'I'm vexed to hear that,' he said levelly. She went to where he stood by the door and took his face between her hands. He tried to jerk his head away impatiently, but she held him, studying the wounds her brother's fists had dealt him. After that initial resistance he stood impassively beneath her touch, face expressionless, eyes fixed on the opposite wall.

There was a large discolouration over his right cheekbone and some swelling at the corner of his mouth where Neil's knuckles had split the skin, but otherwise he was unmarked. When she released him he moved away from her immediately.

'What are you going to do, Kerr?'

'No need to fret about me.' His voice was carefully formal. 'I'm buying Todd Lang's old manufactory and starting up in business on my own account. I went along to see him first thing this morning, for I knew he was hoping to sell.'

She knew the building he meant; a ramshackle old warehouse on the river bank, adjacent to Watson and Bain's mill.

'There are ten spinning jeanies there and I know where I can buy enough roving to put them into production. Not near enough,' he added with faint bitterness 'to fill the mill store-rooms and keep their jeanies working, but enough for my own purposes. And I'll turn my hand to repairing machines for anyone who needs me. We'll get by, the two of us.'

For a breath-stopping moment she thought that he was referring to her. He must have seen it in her face, because he held out a hand to stop her as she began to move to him.

'I'm talking of Philip and me.' His voice was flat and empty. 'How d'you think I'm going to raise the money to buy the place from Todd? I'll have to go cap in hand to the likes of Maxwell King at the Bank. I'll have to go back into debt. I've no room in my life for marriage now, Rowena.'

'I'm more afraid of losing you than I am of living in debt.'

'D'you think I'd allow you to do that?' He came to her then, caught her by the shoulders, his face bleak with anger at the way things had turned out for the two of them. 'D'you think I'd see you wear yourself out and become an old woman before your time as my mother did, because of me?'

Mortally afraid for them both, she clung to him. 'I love you!'

With a groan that was half despair, half anger, he took her into his arms and kissed her; a kiss that told her, more than words ever could, that despite the coolness between them since Elizabeth Melville's appearance, he still loved her. Then he tore himself free and stepped back, his face twisted and tormented.

'Go away, Rowena,' he said harshly. 'Make your own life with someone like Maxwell King — someone who can look after you as you deserve.'

'I'll not leave you like this!'

'You must!' His eyes were slate grey, unrelenting. 'I was a fool to think that things could change, to hope that—'

His voice broke; he turned away from her, his hands gripping the high mantel. She wanted to go to him, but she was afraid of rejection.

'Rowena,' he said carefully at last, 'you know of my father's crimes. I thought I could put them behind me when I paid off his debts, but it seems that it's not going to be as easy as that. I can bring you nothing but grief, and I don't want that to happen. I don't want to see you worn out and old before your time, as my mother was.'

'I don't care, as long as we're together!'

'It seems to me—' he didn't even seem to hear her '—that something – call it fate or fortune or what you will – has taken a great dislike to the Frasers. I'm destined to walk a dark path, whether I like it or not. But at least I can choose to save you from the same misery.'

He swung round on her so suddenly that she flinched. With little regard for courtesy he took her arm, pushed her out into the passageway, and opened the street door. 'I've got my own way to go, and it's a different way from yours. I should never have spoken to you about my feelings. Go home, Rowena!'

The door closed, and she was alone on the step.

*

The Bank was housed in a building that stood in the triangle where Causewayside Street gave way to St Mirren Street, a steep narrow wynd leading to the High Street and Cross. Maxwell King's office was on an upper floor, with a tall narrow window that gave him a good view of the shawl-manufacturers' warehouses clustered on either side of that part of Causewayside.

A smart carriage was waiting outside the door, and as Rowena was about to go into the building Elizabeth Melville emerged. As ever, she was immaculately dressed, this time in a full-length dark velvet cape over matching velvet boots tied, like the cape, with crimson ribbons. Ribbons of the same colour fastened a small bonnet over her dark hair, and her hands were tucked inside a large velvet muff.

Mercifully, she didn't stop to talk, but bowed formally, then stepped into her carriage as Rowena entered the Bank.

'You'll have heard about Kerr Fraser losing his place at the mill?' she asked as soon as she was seated in Maxwell's office.

'The whole town's heard of it. A disgraceful affair – brawling like a street lout for all to see. Fergus must have been beside himself with rage when the news reached his ears.'

Fergus had fallen into a purple-faced fury that seemed set,

until she managed to calm him down, to lead to a fit of apoplexy. Sarah, wringing her hands over Neil and demanding jail, transportation, flogging, and hanging for Kerr Fraser, hadn't helped matters. Now Neil was in bed, playing the invalid, with Sarah and Moira MacKenzie dancing attendance on him.

'The fault lay with Neil as much as with Kerr.' She drew her gloves off and shook her head at his offer of some wine. There were already two fine long-stemmed glasses, one of them still containing a little wine, and a decanter on a silver tray on Maxwell's desk. 'Now Kerr has to find a new way to earn his livelihood. I understand that he's hoping to buy a warehouse with some spinning jeanies.'

'Indeed?' Maxwell watched her, sharp-eyed, making no effort to help her out.

'He intends to ask you for a loan to buy the property and set himself up as proprietor.' She moistened her dry lips. 'I'd look on it as a favour to myself if you'd agree.'

'Don't you think,' Maxwell asked with deceptive mildness, 'that you would be well advised to leave business to the businessmen, and banking to the bankers?'

She met his gaze without flinching. 'Not in this instance.'

'I see.' He got up, went to stand by the window, looking out. 'Since you're so determined to set yourself up as this young man's champion you must persuade me that if I give him the money you're certain he'll ask for, I stand to gain and not lose by the deal.'

He was playing her as an angler played a fish; she knew it, and was angry with him for doing so. But for Kerr's sake she had no choice but to take a deep breath, fix her eyes steadily on his face, in dark profile against the window, and begin to list her arguments in Kerr's favour as clearly as she could.

He heard her out before turning from the window to look at her.

'Does Fergus know you came to me?'

'Nobody knows, and I trust that nobody will ever know.'

'My dear Rowena,' said Maxwell, almost sorrowfully, 'if I am ever to be in need I would give a great deal to have my case pleaded so passionately by such a lovely advocate.'

'Then you'll agree to the loan?'

'However,' he went on smoothly, 'Portia had the wit to realise that a woman should never rely on her beauty as a bargaining point where hard-headed men of business are concerned. If the decision was mine alone I would require a better guarantee than you've been able to give me before recommending that good silver should be handed over to Kerr Fraser.'

Bitter disappointment at his refusal brought a lump to her throat, just as he added, 'But the matter's already out of my hands. Another of the young man's devoted friends has called on me — this time to offer a personal loan and ask me to act as intermediary.'

He took a silver snuff box from its small pocket in his waistcoat, turned it over in his long fingers. 'I'd always thought Kerr Fraser to be a somewhat abrasive young man, but he doesn't seem to lack for well-wishers.'

She stared at him, light-headed with relief. 'Someone's already offered the money? Who is it?'

'Unfortunately I'm not permitted to give you a name. If — when — Mister Fraser comes to me, he's to be given to understand that the loan comes from me,' said Maxwell.

She left the premises feeling cheerful and pleased with life. Kerr's benefactor could be nobody else but Fergus himself, she thought happily, and was almost home before she recalled the used wine glasses on the silver tray, the self-satisfied curve of Elizabeth Melville's lovely mouth as they met outside the Bank.

Her quick, light footsteps slowed. Elizabeth certainly had the money to lend to Kerr. And what better way of influencing her former sweetheart than to buy her way back into his life?

Rowena stopped at the entrance to the Bain driveway. It was unlikely that Fergus, as hard-headed a businessman as Maxwell himself, would hand out money to a young man who had been involved in a brawl in the mill yard. No, it was much more likely to be Elizabeth, she thought, tasting Kerr's last kiss on her lips.

Then she tilted her chin defiantly. Bitter though the thought of a future without him was, she would survive. If fortune did indeed decide these things, then she, too, would be strong enough to go her own way.

*

By the following day the River Cart had succumbed to the freezing weather. The Hammills, the outcrop of rock cutting across the river in the centre of the town to form short falls, turned to a mass of icicles and little boys joyously skated on the wide pool below, where they usually swam each summer.

For the sake of his future relations with his work-force, Fergus Bain felt that he had no option but to continue to pay all the employees thrown out of work by Neil's mistake.

With Neil still playing the invalid and nobody he could fully trust in the counting house, he had the accounts books and ledgers brought to the house to work on them himself.

Rowena, summoned to the library, found him surrounded by paperwork.

'This—' Fergus grumpily stabbed a thick forefinger at a ledger, 'is from the counting-house. And this—' the finger stabbed again, this time at a smaller, slimmer volume '—is the household account book. How is it that your hand appears in both? Or are you going to tell me that your brother ran the kitchen as well as the counting house while I was in Helensburgh? I'll not believe that of the young fool. If it was true we'd have come back to find the house gone to rack and ruin.'

Her heart sank. 'I – I helped Neil now and then, when there was a lot of work—'

'Helped?' said Fergus. 'Now and then? Confound it, lassie, d'you know how to figure or d'you not? That's all I'm asking.'

'I know how to figure. I—' she swallowed. 'I like figuring.'

'Then, since Mistress Cochrane's taken over the housekeeping again and you're no doubt fidgeting to find work for yourself,' growled Fergus, 'you'd best fetch a chair and help me to make sense of these.'

*

From Ibby, Rowena heard that Kerr had obtained his loan, bought the old warehouse, employed a number of cotton-spinners, and set himself up in business.

The bruises and swellings on Neil's face went away and his good looks were restored. He took up horse-riding again and Moira, who had blossomed like a rose during his convalescence, when she visited every day and helped Sarah to pamper him, began to wilt once more, neglected and unhappy.

The cold weather eased towards the end of January. The river ran again, the mill lade was refilled and the great wheel began to revolve.

Colin Gilchrist, one of the mill supervisors, took over Kerr's duties and Neil went back to the counting house.

But memories and grievances took longer to heal than cuts and bruises. Colin came to the house to see Fergus, shuffling his feet and twisting his cap between two calloused hands, to report that Neil's presence was in danger of sparking off more trouble.

'By God—' Fergus spluttered, thumping the arm of his chair. 'You'll tell the lot of them from me to stop their muttering and get on with their work! If I'd the proper use of my confounded legs, I'd soon put them to rights!'

'D'you think it's as easy as all that?' Colin, caught between the devil and the ocean, forgot about diplomacy. 'I'm telling you, Mister Bain, the lad's got a way of talking to folk that'll see murder done if he's not careful!'

'Nonsense, man!'

'You know fine that your mill workers aren't given to being difficult – as long as they're treated like human beings and not dirt under someone's feet. And there's no sense in thinking things'll improve, not with feelings the way they are in the town just now, and young Philip Fraser speaking out against Neil whenever he gets the chance.'

'There's another one that's looking for trouble – Philip Fraser!'

'Aye. He's not got his brother's common sense, more's the pity. But it's not Philip we're talking about. I'm telling you, Mister Bain – you'll have to do something!'

He went away, plodding down the drive, his thin, honest face twisted with worry. After some thought Fergus sent for his store-man, and for the first time since his children went to live at Carriagehill Ewan Lindsay walked along the driveway and took a firm hold of the gleaming brass door-knocker.

'You'll take a glass with me, Ewan?' Fergus asked when his visitor had been shown into the library by Ibby, her eyes almost popping from her head with surprise and curiosity.

'Aye,' said Ewan.

'Thank God for that,' Fergus grunted. 'At last we're talking the same language again, you and me.'

Their meeting was long, and honest on both sides. Ewan knew his son far better than Neil realised, even to the passion for horse-riding that Neil shared with Mistress Elizabeth Melville. He had decided, during his walk to the house, that the time had come for plain speaking if the mill was to be saved.

Fergus, who had always had great respect for his store-man and had deeply regretted the long years of widowhood and re-marriage, when Ewan had locked himself away from his fellow-men, listened and learned and took advice. Then he had a meeting with Mister MacKenzie and, finally, with Neil himself.

His most difficult moment came when he had to face his wife and tell her what had been decided. Sarah had set her heart on Neil taking over the mill like a true son; but on the other hand, she had to agree on reflection, Mister MacKenzie's shawl manu-factory was prospering. And once Neil and Moira were wed and settled in London, where Neil was to represent the MacKenzie interests, Sarah would be able to visit them and sample the English ways of life. And, of course, there was still the wedding to arrange – Sarah gave in, and the matter was settled.

Within the space of a day Neil, secretly relieved at being rid of the mill responsibilities, had moved to the MacKenzie ware-house, to work under his future father-in-law's supervision.

Mistress Melville had little difficulty in finding another com-panion to accompany her when she rode out in the afternoons, and Rowena, to her astonishment and delight, was set to deal-ing with the accounts again.

'But only in the meantime,' Sarah stipulated. 'It's not a seemly task for a young lady. Once the wedding's over, Rowena, we must see to it that you become properly introduced into society.'

The wedding was planned for July. By that time, Mister Mac-Kenzie estimated, Neil would be ready to make the move to London.

The snow on the braes melted and cold clear water gushed down the ravines and into the Cart. Fresh green grass broke through the earth. The trees took on pleasant green blurred outlines.

Kerr Fraser and Rowena Lindsay set out on their different roads, each determined to make a success of their ventures. They occasionally met in the streets as they went about their lives, and each time they bowed, and passed on, and kept their thoughts to themselves.

And the revolution that had been simmering all winter behind closed doors began to stir again.

XXII

As the spring flowers covered the moors round the town with drifts of colour, notices and proclamations began to blossom on doors and walls, calling on the workers to rise and fight against tyranny.

Many of the Paisley looms fell silent, and it seemed that at last the broken pieces of Staffordshire plate were to be re-united and the country plunged into a revolution every bit as bloody as the French troubles had been.

Meetings were held in weaving-shops, at street corners, and on the moors, and Philip Fraser flitted from one to the other, urging the men on, whipping any resentment he found into white-hot fever.

Ibby was sick with worry about him. 'Kerr can't do a thing with him now − it's as if he's being eaten up inside with these feelings of his. He'll end up in the jail if he's not careful, and then what'll I do?'

'Ibby, would you not be wise to let Philip go his own way, whatever that may be, and find your happiness with someone else?' Rowena was driven to suggest at last.

Her friend looked at her with eyes that were red-rimmed from weeping, but shocked nevertheless.

'Leave him? How can I make my life with anyone else when

it's Philip I love?' she said with simple directness, and Rowena, thinking of Kerr and the great gulf that had opened between them, fell silent.

The town waited. There seemed to be a lack of leadership, with some men maintaining that the notices heralding the revolution had been posted by Government agents bent on setting a trap, and others insisting that they were a genuine call to arms.

In March the militia made a house to house search for illicit weapons. Quickly though they moved word hurried before them, and a group of men scooped up the pikes and pistols that awaited the civil war and carried them off to a secret cache in the braes.

Paisley men born and bred, they knew the terrain so well that they could have found their way in total darkness; they were cheerfully confident, as they struck further into the countryside, that they could outrun any troops who came after them.

Even so, some half-dozen armed men, Philip among them, took up the rear, ready to fight if need be.

They had almost reached the place where the arms were to be hidden when a group of horsemen were sighted. At once the party melted into the folds and tucks of the hillsides, away from the beaten track the horsemen were using.

Philip, full-length on the grass, wriggled his fingers until the butt of his pistol lay securely in the palm of his hand. The old excitement that had gripped him when he was soldiering tingled in the pit of his stomach.

The man beside him lifted his head cautiously to peep over the rim of the slope where they lay, then ducked down again. 'Ach, it's not the militia at all,' he reported in a whisper. 'It's just a group of men, likely riding over to Barrhead. We'll let them pass then be on our way.'

The ground beneath Philip's cheek vibrated to a measured beat, telling of horses being ridden at a walk. He heard deep voices, the occasional burst of laughter. A group of young dandies were doubtless on their way over to some howff where they could drink and play cards.

He lifted his head to watch them go by and his eyes narrowed as he recognised Neil Lindsay among them. At sight of the man who had imperiously ordered him out of the mill yard slow anger began to course through Philip's muscles, tensing them.

The group drew level with the hidden men, then passed, Neil and another man slightly behind the others. Philip watched, his gaze fixed on Neil as though the sight of the slight figure sitting its horse with casual grace, the handsome face relaxed in laughter, mesmerised him.

Neil, busy talking to his companion, failed to see a low branch in time and it swept his hat from his dark head. He had to rein in his mount and get down to retrieve it while the other man laughed and rode on.

Without conscious bidding Philip's arm moved, the pistol lifting until he was looking at Neil Lindsay through the sights. Neil remounted as the man who lay beside Philip turned his head to speak and saw taut intention in his companion's thin face and in the finger that was already curving round the firing mechanism.

For a second he stared, unable to believe his eyes; then he lunged forward just as Philip, Neil still well and truly in his sights, fired the pistol.

*

Neil returned home shaken and bone-white with rage. The ball from his would-be assassin's pistol had gone close enough to tear the sleeve of his thick coat and break the skin beneath it; his only other injuries were some scratches and bruises sustained when his horse reared in fright at the noise, throwing him off.

Neither he nor his companions had been able to identify the handful of men who had risen from hiding places and fled while the startled horse-riders were still trying to grasp what had happened. But Neil was in no doubt as to the identity of the man who had tried to kill him. Philip Fraser, a former soldier, had threatened publicly to shoot him. Philip Fraser had tried to make good his threat.

Philip was nowhere to be found. His brother, gaunt and hard-eyed, denied any knowledge of his whereabouts. The house in Barclay Street was searched, as were all the wanted man's usual haunts, without success.

Ibby crept about her duties like a ghost, until Rowena could bear her unhappiness no longer.

'You know where he is, don't you?'

Ibby's eyes, no longer bright little buttons, slid evasively away from her friend's face. 'He's probably gone to England, or mebbe to the North, or—'

'If he has, he's a fool. The militia'll get him eventually. He'd be well advised to take a boat and go far away to a place where he can make a new life in safety. Somewhere like America.'

'How can we – he—' Ibby corrected herself hastily, '—manage that?'

Rowena flourished the newspaper she had been studying when the maid came in to dust. 'There's a ship leaving Greenock next Saturday, bound for America. Philip – if you only knew where he was – could be got to it somehow.'

Ibby sniffed and rubbed her eyes, sore from weeping, with the back of one hand. 'And what would we – he – use for money?'

Fergus had insisted on giving Rowena wages for the work she had done as house-keeper and book-keeper. 'I've got a little. Not much, but enough to pay for two people's passage. For goodness' sake, Ibby,' said Rowena, suddenly losing patience with the game they were playing. 'Go to him, wherever he is, and tell him you're going together to America, where he'll be safe.'

'But—' said Ibby feebly '—why would you help Philip when he near killed your own brother?'

'I'm not helping him, I'm helping you.' Rowena began the sentence briskly, but on the last words her voice shook and tears came to her own eyes. 'And I'll miss you so much, Ibby!' she said, and the two of them fell sobbing into each other's arms.

Easy though the plan had sounded when she spoke of it to Ibby, Rowena had no notion of how to smuggle Philip from Paisley to Greenock; then as good fortune would have it Colin Gilchrist, the man who had reluctantly agreed to take over Kerr's duties in the mill, came to her on the following afternoon when she was in Fergus's small private room over the counting house.

'One of the spinning jeanies on the top floor needs seeing to and I've no notion what's amiss with the thing.'

She was supposed to be working out the wages, but instead she had been trying to solve Philip's problem.

'Can none of the others repair it?'

He shook his head gloomily. 'I wish to God Kerr Fraser was here. He'd a way with machinery that nobody else has. I tell you, Miss Rowena, I've not got the stomach for this work. I'd be happier back in my old position as overseer.'

'D'you mean you want us to find a new manager?'

'I'd be obliged,' he said awkwardly. 'There's no sense in keeping on a task I'm not fitted to do.'

She sighed. 'Very well, I'll speak to Mister Bain.'

She went back to her work as he turned towards the door, then the quill fell from her fingers as an idea blazed into her mind. 'Colin?'

He turned back to her, eyebrows raised.

'Is it true that you're one of the men who owns the *Union of Paisley*?'

'Aye, it's true.' Colin's face was suddenly wary. 'And if you've anything comical to say about it, Miss Rowena, I'd best tell you now that it'll not go down well as far as I'm concerned.'

The *Union*, a sixteen-foot sailed pleasure boat, had been bought by a group of Paisley men the year before. The River Cart was tidal, opening to the mouth of the River Clyde; its waters were deep enough to give passage to cargo ships carrying goods to and from Paisley, which had two harbours. An ideal situation, the men had decided, for a fishing boat.

On her maiden voyage, a fishing trip to Gourock, the *Union* had gone aground on a sandbank off Port-Glasgow, an adventure that her owners and crew had not been able to live down. Whenever any of them were spotted within hearing distance some local wit or other was certain to make comments about the port of Paisley and its fishing fleet. The boat was moored at Cartvale harbour, not far from the centre of town.

'I'm not about to tease you, Colin.' Rowena rose and went to close the door, which was ajar. 'I'm going to ask you if you'd be willing to go fishing on Friday night, and take some folk with you—'

*

On Friday night the two girls walked demurely through the streets, to all intents and purposes on their way to visit friends. A small bag containing all Ibby possessed in the world had already been taken down to the harbour by Colin.

Through Ibby, who acted as go-between, Philip had insisted that for his own safety Kerr wasn't to know what was going on. Rowena had agreed, but as she and Ibby went past his warehouse she saw that the windows were lit, and stopped on the footpath.

'Ibby, it's not right that Kerr should miss the chance to say goodbye to his brother. I'm going in to tell him that Philip's going away. Wait for me—'

She could hear the spinning jeanies clacking as she picked her way across a yard that was cluttered with timber and boxes. The door swung open beneath her hand and she stepped into the big shed, lit by lamps hung from the walls.

Kerr was by one of the machines, arms folded across his chest, watching its progress with his brows knotted together in a thoughtful scowl.

He looked up as the door swung shut behind her; a mixture of expressions passed over his face, but she couldn't be sure, because of the pattern of light and shadow in the place, whether pleasure was among them.

For herself, the sweet pain of seeing him again was almost more than she could bear for a moment. She hadn't realised, busy as she was with her work at the mill and the nervous excitement of arranging to get Philip and Ibby away safely, how much she was missing him. It took all the self-control she could summon up to face him when he reached her.

'What are you doing here?' The question was abrupt, harsh – and the slight surge of anger it woke in her helped to give her own voice a crisp impersonal edge.

'I've come to give you the chance to say your farewells to your brother, Kerr Fraser.' Then she explained swiftly, low-voiced, making sure that there was no chance of being overheard by the spinners.

He reached for his hat without wasting time on questions. Within a minute or two they had joined Ibby, waiting nervously at the gate, and were on their way to the river, passing groups of militia here and there as they went.

The soldiers went by without comment — there was nothing suspicious about three respectable-looking young people walking through the town, the girls arm in arm, the man escorting them.

Colin and his friends were already at the harbour, preparing the boat for its fishing trip. They had been close-mouthed about it and the sight-seers who would normally have been at the harbour to watch them go were missing.

At first there was no sign of Philip. Ibby looked about, wringing her hands nervously; then a figure stepped from the dark shadow of a hut nearby, and Philip Fraser was with them.

There was little time for farewells. Ibby and Rowena hugged each other briefly before Ibby, tears on her cheeks, was helped down the ladder and into the boat. Kerr and Philip exchanged a few swift words and a handshake, then after a moment's hesitation Philip went over to Rowena.

'I'm obliged to you for what you've done,' he muttered, adding swiftly, 'I'll make certain you get your money back, every penny of it.'

'Just see that Ibby's looked after.' She watched him go nimbly down the ladder, despite his bad leg, and take his place beside Ibby, who immediately took his hand in hers, holding it as though she would never again let it go.

The mooring rope was cast off, the men took up their oars, and the *Union of Paisley* swung out into the river and began to slip down towards the Clyde, and Greenock, and safety.

Rowena and Kerr watched in silence until there was nothing to be seen but the water, grey silk in the darkness, and nothing to hear but the river's lap against the quay.

'I'll see that you get home safely,' he said at last, and put his hand on her arm, turning her towards the street.

It was a silent journey, with both of them occupied by thoughts of Philip and Ibby travelling together to an unknown future.

Rowena glanced up at her companion once or twice, but he

was staring straight ahead, his face hard to make out in the darkness.

When they stopped at the Bains' gate she said, to break the awkward silence, 'They'll be fine.'

'They'll have to be. It's his last chance and he's got a long hard road to go.'

'Ibby's with him — he's not alone any more. It'll make all the difference, being together.'

'I'm not so sure. He'd mebbe have been better on his own, at least until he had something to offer her,' Kerr said slowly, and she knew with a sinking heart that the determination to go his own way was still strong in him.

'How are you going to explain Ibby's disappearance?'

'Mistress Bain's mortally afraid of sickness. I'll tell her that Ibby took ill at her mother's house, and she's staying there till her fever's gone. That'll do for a few days, and after that I'll be as surprised as anyone else to hear that Ibby's gone from the town.'

She held out her hand and he took it in his. 'Thank you for escorting me home, Kerr,' she said formally.

'It's me that has to thank you for all you've done for my brother. I'm in your debt.'

Despair and frustration prompted her to say, in a voice sharp-edged with misery, 'Don't be. I'd not want to bring any more debts on your shoulders.'

Then she turned and marched along the drive to the house, wanting to look over her shoulder to see if he was watching her, yet afraid to in case she discovered that he had gone.

XXIII

In March Elizabeth Melville stunned all of Paisley by holding a gathering at her rooms in Garthland Place to mark her return to Edinburgh and her betrothal to Maxwell King.

Sarah, who had travelled to Helensburgh only two days earlier, hastened back to Carriagehill when word of the invitation reached her, her blue eyes almost bulging from her plump face with astonishment.

'There's no time to have a new dress made, I'll have to go in my blue silk. Why didn't you sent word as soon as you learned the way the wind lay, Rowena?'

'I knew nothing about it — not even Mistress Mackenzie had any idea that the two of them planned to marry,' Rowena protested. It was quite true. A few days after Philip Fraser and Ibby slipped out of Paisley, Maxwell had called on her and requested, with an air of embarrassment, that he be released from any understanding that they may have had. Rowena, who had been thrown into a state of alarm by his visit, and was convinced that he had called to make a formal proposal and insist on an answer, had agreed to the request with a beaming relief that had obviously disconcerted Maxwell even further. She had not asked why he had changed his mind, and he had not offered any explanation.

The houses in Garthland Place, on the other side of the river, were among the finest in Paisley. Elizabeth's temporary home consisted of a series of huge, high-ceilinged apartments, warmed on this chill wet night by fires in all the big fireplaces, lit by countless candelabra, bright with curtains and cushions and rugs that Elizabeth had had brought over from Edinburgh.

She herself was at her most striking, her vivid dark beauty set off by a gown of virginal white with bunches of silver ribbon, and silver thread embroidery.

The betrothal had come as a surprise to everybody. Watching, with cool amusement, her guests' attempts to restrain their burning curiosity, she explained that she and her daughter planned to return to Edinburgh within a few days. Maxwell would join them there once he had settled his business affairs in Paisley. Maxwell, said Elizabeth with a contented smile, was thinking of entering into politics after the wedding.

As the evening wore on she made a point of seeking Rowena out, taking her arm and leading her into a corner of the drawing room.

'Maxwell assures me that he asked you in the proper manner to free him from the — understanding — that existed between you, my dear.'

'Indeed he did, though I'd never thought us to have an understanding.'

Elizabeth laughed lightly. 'Even so, he was determined to observe all the proprieties. Dear Maxwell, he has delightfully strong opinions where women are concerned. Mill girls are only there to be used and forgotten, but ladies must be treated well. That's what has always attracted me to him. That's why I came back.'

'He knew you before?'

'Oh, yes.' Elizabeth turned to look at her future husband, who was deep in conversation with Fergus. 'Of course, he didn't remember me. I was only one of his mill girls in those days. By the way, I invited Kerr here tonight, but it seems that he's too busy with his new manufactory to dabble in society. Such a pity.'

Long dark lashes swept over her violet eyes, then lifted again to allow her to study Rowena.

'He called in person to proffer his regrets, and stayed for all of an hour. He still has a certain charm — I think Anne quite fell in love with him.'

'He saw her?'

'Of course. And so shall you, for I promised her that she should be presented to my friends before the evening ends.'

'Does Kerr know that you advanced the money he borrowed?'

For once, Elizabeth Melville looked taken aback. 'Did Maxwell tell you? No—' she answered her own question. 'I believe you thought it out by yourself. You have a shrewd mind, Rowena Lindsay. No, Kerr doesn't know and there's no reason why he ever should. Now I must go and fetch Anne.'

Rowena detained her with a hand on the white silk-clad arm. 'Why did you give him the money?'

'Why?' Elizabeth deliberated for a moment. 'If I was of a romantic nature I might say that it was in memory of the days when Kerr and I were sweethearts. But romance has no part in my life.'

Her eyes, searching Rowena's face, lit up with malicious glee. 'Though I do believe you thought that was the reason. Poor Rowena, how jealous you must have been!'

'No,' Rowena lied, and knew that Elizabeth Melville wasn't deceived.

'You'd no need to fret, my dear, your Kerr was never the man for me. Oh, he's ambitious in his own way, but he'll be content enough to stay in Paisley and raise sons to follow him in his business. Maxwell, on the other hand, is ruthless as well as successful. I've a hunger for politics, and he shall be the one to satisfy it for me.'

Her violet eyes grew hazy, looking beyond the walls of the room to something that only she could see.

'Perhaps one day, through Maxwell, I shall play my part in shaping Britain.'

'Then why make the loan to Kerr?' Rowena persisted and her hostess, brought back to the present from her golden dreams of the future, laughed.

'Why? Because I knew that your brother would be incensed when he discovered that Kerr had found his feet again. And Neil is quite beautiful when he's angry. Now I really must fetch Anne.'

Anne, a pretty little girl, pale from her illness, but remarkably self-assured in company, was duly brought in to be fussed over by her mother's guests.

Rowena, who had awaited her appearance nervously, took one look at the child and felt a wave of relief sweep over her. Anne had no look of Kerr Fraser at all. Her pretty, determined little mouth and her rich black hair gave her the look of her mother, but her eyes were brown in a long-jawed face.

'Why,' Mistress MacKenzie twittered, 'She has something of the look of her new papa! You shall be a real family! What a delightful co-incidence!'

'Delightful,' Elizabeth agreed smoothly, and Rowena, gazing at Maxwell with startled comprehension, saw that he looked just a little disconcerted.

*

The revolution died before it had been truly born. Those who claimed that the notices urging action had been posted by Government agents setting a trap for the workers proved to be right. Gradually Paisley settled back to its normal routine.

Neil and Moira married, and went south to their new home in London. Sarah set about the task of looking for a suitable husband for Rowena. The new works manager Fergus had taken on proved to be unsatisfactory, and was dismissed.

'We need to get Kerr Fraser back,' Fergus announced.

Rowena's heart still felt a faint twinge of pain whenever Kerr's name was mentioned. 'From what I hear, he's doing fine,' she said shortly.

'Aye, and I'd as soon he was doing fine on my account as on his. Have a word with him. Rowena.'

'I will not!'

He glowered at her, but there was an upward tuck at each corner of his mouth. Neil's marriage and departure had been something like removing a stone from a shoe; now Rowena and Fergus had a comfortable, affectionate relationship that served them well, especially as far as the mill was concerned.

A similar affection had sprung up between herself and Ewan, who tramped along to Carriagehill at least once a week now, to play chess with Fergus. It was ironic that the child had had no father, and the woman had two.

'I thought we'd agreed that it's your place to see to hiring folk for the mill,' Fergus reminded her now.

'We can manage fine without Kerr Fraser. If you want him, speak to him yourself.'

'I doubt,' said Fergus dryly, 'if I could persuade him the way you could.'

'I doubt if anyone could make that man change his mind.'

For answer, he picked up a paper from the library desk and handed it to her. She unfolded it and scanned it with growing disbelief. It was Kerr Fraser's loan note; Maxwell King's name had been scored out and replaced by her own.

'Maxwell brought it to me before he left for Edinburgh.' Fergus looked pleased with himself. 'It seems that for some reason it was a personal loan, made out with the Bank. I bought it from him.'

'But—' she dropped the paper as though it was burning hot, '—why put my name on it?'

'Call it a wedding gift,' he said slyly. 'I hear there's a marriageable Honourable in Helensburgh. Speaking for myself, though, I think Kerr Fraser would suit you better. I might add that Ewan's of the same mind as me.'

'Are you talking about a husband or a works manager?' she asked acidly. 'Mebbe you should propose to the man yourself, on behalf of the mills.'

'It's your name that's on the paper.' He picked it up again, held it out to her. 'The second payment on his loan's due next week. That's when you can persuade him to throw his lot in with Watson and Bain again – and with Rowena Lindsay too.'

'You can do your own persuading.'

'Pride sits badly on young shoulders.'

'Tell that to Kerr Fraser.' She slammed the account ledger shut with hands that shook slightly, and got to her feet.

Out in the garden she savagely ripped a few weeds from the flower-beds then fetched scissors and a basket, remembering as the torment within her heart calmed that she had intended to cut some roses to put in the parlour. Fergus liked the scent of them in the house.

The rose-bushes were rich with blooms. As Rowena carefully selected the best and laid them in her basket Fergus's parting remark went through her head. She remembered, too, what Ewan had said. 'Pride's all very well, lass, but it makes a poor bed-fellow, specially when you're young and the blood's coursing through your body.'

The air about her, as she stood in the sunlit garden, was fragrant with the perfume of the white and pink and red and yellow and peach-coloured roses in her hands. Bees bumbled happily from flower to flower on a nearby bush.

Thoughts of Kerr filled her mind; her longing for him hadn't altered, even though she had worked hard to erase it, ever since the night the two of them had watched Philip and Ibby leave.

'It would serve him right if I did marry the marriageable Honourable,' she said to a sparrow that fluttered down to the path nearby and watched her hopefully.

And all at once she knew that she would never forgive herself if she let that happen.

*

He came up the stairs like an enraged bull, taking the steps two and three at a time and bursting into Fergus's private office above the counting-house without bothering to knock.

Rowena, who had been awaiting this moment all morning, and had been sitting before the same page in the ledger, quill in hand, for a full two hours without touching pen to paper, tried to look mildly surprised.

'You tricked me!' Kerr threw the paper he carried onto the desk before her. She laid down her dry quill, picked up the loan note, and studied it carefully before looking up.

'I take it you've come to make the interest payment, Mister Fraser?'

'Make the—?' Words failed him, then he rallied, dragging a handful of coins from his pocket and scattering them across the ledger.

'Aye, I'll make the payment — and I'll see to it that you get every penny owing to you before the year's out, supposing—'

'Supposing you've to borrow the money to do it from someone else?'

'I'll not be indebted to a woman!'

She swept the coins aside with a movement of her hand. 'I don't see why that should make any difference. Why shouldn't women deal with money? We're expected to make the wages stretch to feed the family. We're expected to buy wisely at the market. Women, Mister Fraser, are just as able as men. Look at your own mother, for one.'

'And look at how the worry of it killed her,' he said stiffly.

'I don't intend to let that happen to me. I've a proposal to put to you — with Mister Bain's full knowledge and approval.'

He watched her warily. In the months since they had last spoken he'd lost the gaunt look that had come on him while he was worrying over Philip, though his face was still shaped by the hard angles and firm lines that she'd always thought handsome.

There was a down droop, though, to his mouth; she had to resist the urge to go to him and smooth it out with her fingers.

Instead, she got up and walked to the window overlooking the yard. From here she could see part of the mill's bulk, and the corner of the yard by the bridge over the river.

The great water-wheel was out of her line of vision, but she knew that if she moved across to the window on the other wall she would catch the glitter of water-drops now and then as the iron buckets lifted out of the lade, one after another.

'Well?' Kerr prompted from where he still stood by the desk.

'We — Watson and Bain — want to buy your manufactory. The land's adjacent to ours, and we could make good use of your spinning jeanies too. And of course, if you sold to us you could discharge the debt that's suddenly become so distasteful to you.'

He had recovered from his first rage; now his voice was quiet, iron-hard. 'You think I'd be content to give up a business that's begun to prosper and start again, just to suit Watson and Bain?'

'You'd not be required to start again. You'd take charge of the mill as the manager, and take a partnership as well.'

There was a brief silence, then 'Who'd be responsible for the counting house?' he wanted to know.

'I would.' She could just catch her own reflection in the window pane; she had dressed carefully for this meeting, choosing a simple dark-green gown that flattered her slender figure and her auburn hair.

'I'm not certain we could work well together.'

'I don't see why not.' She took a deep breath, to steady her voice. 'We'd move your spinning jeanies to the mill and build a new counting house and schoolroom where your manufactory stands now. The children need better accommodation than they have at present.'

'And what of this building?'

'It's—' she faltered, regained her composure with an effort, '—it's been a beautiful home in its time. I'd like to turn it into a home again.'

'I heard,' he said, 'that you were leaving Paisley. I heard that you're soon to be betrothed to some titled man in Helensburgh.'

For a brief moment Rowena thought ill of Sarah and her silly gossiping tongue. Then she turned and smiled brilliantly at him.

'As to that, I've not decided yet.'

'You should accept him. You deserve—' Kerr stopped, head bent over the loan note he was turning over and over in his hands. Then he looked up again.

'You deserve so much more than I could give you, Rowena.'

She laughed, a trifle shakily. 'We never seem to be able to agree, Kerr. I'd be more than content to settle for whatever you could give me.'

"Then you'd be a fool — and so would I, to think that that would be enough,' he said with angry violence in his voice. 'I thank Providence every day that I stopped myself from asking you to take me as your husband there and then, just after my mother died. If I had, and if you'd accepted, look at the misery you'd have been put through!'

'So you think I've been happy, knowing all you've suffered, and not able to help you?'

'I thought you were helping me, by your way of it,' he said bitterly, brushing the fingers of one hand against the paper. 'You're anxious to free me from my debts and to get me a partnership with Watson and Bain!'

'You truly think that Fergus Bain would offer you a partnership because of my feelings for you? He wants you back for his own sake, Kerr — and if you've any sense you'll admit that your future lies with this mill.'

And with me, she wanted to add. With me by your side, for the rest of our lives. But she held back. Kerr must make up his own mind, and she, now that she had declared herself as openly as she could, must give him the freedom to walk away from her for ever, if he so decided.

As though reading her mind, he put the loan note down and went to the door.

'You can tell Mister Bain that I'll give him my answer within the week.'

'Kerr—' she said as he was going out, 'Philip's gone, your father's debts are honoured. There's nothing to keep you from living your own life — nothing but foolish pride that'll destroy you if you let it.'

He hesitated, his fingers on the door-handle, then went out without answering or looking at her.

Rowena gathered up the coins Kerr had thrown down before her, and put them in a neat pile to one side. Then she tore the document he had brought into small pieces and laid them tidily beside the money.

She glanced up at the elegant, dirty ceiling over her head. The building could indeed be turned back into a fine house, with Kerr's father's grand portrait hanging in the downstairs parlour, and the room she stood in converted into a nursery—

Back at the window, she watched until Kerr's tall figure came into view, striding quickly across the yard to the bridge.

He began to cross the bridge, moving away from her with a decisive step that, even as she watched, faltered and slowed.

She caught her breath, felt her heart give a strange double thump against her ribs as Kerr swept his tall hat from his head and looked up at the old house, his eyes searching for, and finding, the window where she stood motionless as the subject in a portrait.

The breeze ruffled his russet hair. Although the window was dirty and the way the sunlight fell meant that he probably couldn't make her out behind the glass, she was convinced that their eyes met, and held. Then Kerr began to walk swiftly back across the bridge. The hat fell from his hand, discarded and forgotten. It rolled to the edge between the railings, hesitated, then fell over into the water below.

Kerr began to run.

As he disappeared from view Rowena turned from the window and went out into the upper hall.

Below, the big front door swung back on its hinges, then

came the impatient sound of his footsteps hurrying up the staircase.

She caught up her skirts and ran, her feet barely skimming the treads, to meet him.

Bibliography

The Paisley Thread

Matthew Blair

Statistical Account of Scotland,
Volume VII The Paisley Pamphlets

Renfrew District
Libraries Services